When Fireflies Sing

Christene Houston

*To Jon,
my favorite Uncle.
♡ you!
Christene Houston*

When Fireflies Sing
Copyright © 2017 Christene Houston
All rights reserved

The book contained herein constitutes a copyrighted work and may not be reproduced, transmitted, down-loaded, or stored in or introduced into an information storage and retrieval system in any form or by any means, whether electronic or mechanical, now known or hereinafter invented, without the express written permission of the copyright owner, except in the case of brief quotation embodied in critical articles and reviews.

This book is a work of fiction. The names, characters, places, and incidents are products of the writer's imagination or have been used fictitiously and are not to be construed as real. Any resemblance to persons, living or dead, actual events, locales or organizations is entirely coincidental.

Interior book design by Bob Houston eBook Formatting

To Michelle

Midnight milk runs, silly stories, my first duet partner

Sisters, friends, trouble-makers

I look forward to the adventures ahead.

Chapter One

Helen: WHERE ARE YOU, IZZY! JASPER IS GETTING REALLY UPSET!! I CAN'T BELIEVE YOU WOULD BE SO INCONSIDERATE WHEN THE CONTRACT IS ON THE LINE!!

Liz: How could you duck out of this stupid dinner. You suck!

Jen: You owe me five prime-time tweets for covering for you, Iz.

Jasper: ...

Isabelle Atkins, the youngest sister in the Atkins social media dynasty, watched her phone light up like a firework display. Texts ricocheted between her sisters who took turns whining and scolding. There were bright punctuations from her mother—always in shouty caps—declaring her untold suffering. Isabelle watched it all with growing indifference. She knew her mother was only concerned about the media image they were presenting at the high-profile restaurant. An absent child could easily be twisted into family discord.

Isabelle took a deep breath of the city air around her and instantly regretted it. It smelled of smog, remnants of an over-warm late spring day, and the water beneath the bridge she stood on. She would not miss it for a second. Not when her lungs had grown up on fresh country air.

Sometimes she could still smell it, even in the city, and that scent of fresh hay, sunshine, and growing things tugged at her heart in a way that the city never could. Other times, if she closed her eyes tightly and really tried, she could even see the fireflies that danced across the meadow backing up to Grandma's house. There was something mesmerizing in the bob and sway of their gentle light.

False starlight fell on her hair which was cropped to her shoulders with a slip of bangs that swept across her forehead, brushing her full lashes. Dark. Dark hair, dark eyes. Her reflection was one she wasn't used to seeing after months of false pretenses.

Those deep brown eyes watched the phone where it sat on the bridge hand rail.

Four inches of steel.

That was the width of the city bridge railing. Her phone was the latest and greatest that technology could offer. It was the first thing she saw every morning and often fell from her hand late into the night when she dozed off mid-tweet. It was usually shrouded in a case bedazzled in jewels and gems that would probably go for enough to buy her a new car, if she wanted one.

She'd tucked that case into an envelope that would reach her attorney with instructions to sell it and donate the proceeds to her favorite charity. A satisfied smile twisted her lips at the thought.

With every notification, the phone vibrated to life, inching itself innocently from the center of the railing and ever closer to it's doom. Dark, rushing water hurried below, slurping up the sounds of the cars that whizzed by behind her. Tiny as she was at only five feet—and painfully thin—she hid perfectly behind the post that separated the walkway from the road. It felt deliciously sinful to be completely unnoticed on a night like this.

In the little town of Gunlock, there'd been a bridge where she could go and think. It was a place she resorted to when big decisions needed to be made. Tonight, the choice was final. Her time on the bridge now was for reflection and a last goodbye to the life she knew.

For the past seven years, the Atkins family had worked their way up from absolutely nothing to a worldwide empire. Everyone who was anyone knew the lovely Atkins sisters.

Elizabeth—with her sharp eye for fashion—set trends whenever she stepped out of her posh city penthouse. She'd launched an online clothing boutique that specialized in selling her one-of-a-kind pieces. A chance encounter with an A-lister had catapulted her from unknown to having her name dropped on the red carpet.

Jennifer was the beauty of the family. She modeled and created a coveted makeup line that sold out the moment it was released. Men hit on her wherever she went.

Isabelle was the musician in the family. Now, she folded her arms around herself, though the bite of Spring had long since been tamed by the promise of summer. She thought wryly about her music career.

Yes, she was the musician, singing top ten pop songs that all the radio stations played. But the truth was, none of the songs she actually wrote had ever seen the light of day. Oh, what had Helen called them? A bit too sweet for the Atkins team? Isabelle smirked as her phone edged one corner off the railing.

For three years, she'd tried to be what they wanted, but she was done trying.

The wedding contract had put the final nail in the coffin, but the other nails had been driven in one by one from the moment she returned to the city and found her family almost unrecognizable.

As a girl, they'd all shared the same dark hair and eyes. Now, her sisters changed their hair through a rainbow of hues, depending on their social commitments for the week. Their wardrobes were runway ready, and Isabelle's stomach still knotted at the dollar amount that went into clothing them alone. It was obscene to spend so much on things they wore once and never again. As a girl who grew up with an affinity for thrift store shopping, that had never settled well with her.

Even still, she felt she could have found a way to endure if it hadn't been for the contracts her mother, or

Helen, as the girls were given to calling her, had proposed that first week she was home. She'd been too shocked to speak up, even as her stomach sank, watching her sister, Liz, sign on the dotted line without so much as an argument.

The contract specified who Liz would marry, how long the marriage had to remain intact, and how many children the union would produce, even detailing how the whole thing should end for optimum press coverage.

Liz was to be married to a business mogul with a contract that stipulated three kids and a healthy gouge of his assets when they divorced at eight years under a media storm. The resulting alimony would be just the thing to launch a new maternity line alongside her current high fashion boutique after the sacrifice of motherhood took her down a notch. At this point, Liz was on year three and baby number one. So far, pregnancy was her least favorite shape.

Jen's marriage to a hot football star had fallen apart long before her contract came due, but she did have her daughter, Constellation, to show for it. The publicity on that short-lived marriage had been a shower of poison arrows. Everyone seemed delighted to tear the most beautiful Atkins sister to shreds with headlines like "Ice Queen Loses Her King" and "Beauty or a Beast?" Pregnant with her baby girl and devastated by her ex-husband's abusive tendencies and philandering ways, Jenni had shrunk away from the spotlight for a time.

Spending her teen years in a small town under the tutelage of her Grandma made Isabelle far more aware of the ridiculousness of the situation. After watching Jen suffer through her marriage and the subsequent hell of a divorce, Isabelle gathered her courage to resist Helen's attempts to line her up as the next tribute.

Helen had a prospect in mind and a contract laid out. It made Isabelle's protests feel like screaming into a hurricane. Nothing she said made it through the frenzy of whipping winds.

Jasper, one of the Brandon triplets and soaring high on a soap opera deal that capitalized on three handsome men who looked alike, was her intended.

Forget that blondes weren't her thing.

Forget his low opinion of fidelity.

Forget that his smile had the effect of bad pork on her stomach.

Oy. Times three, since where one brother was, the others were happily tagging along. In the unfortunate collection of events where she'd been forced into the brothers' company, Isabelle was pretty sure they'd taken turns trying to get her alone. None of them had succeeded in being anything but sleazy. Her stomach did a memorial somersault at the thought.

Isabelle's contract was simple, according to Helen. Five years of marriage, two kids—one boy and one girl—and then she was free. Then there was the delightful fine print Isabelle had not been stupid enough to ignore. The tiny clause that said Jasper could see other women as long as he kept it under wraps from the media. Unless, that is, they needed a boost in the ratings, and then he could be caught in an illicit affair, followed by lavish repentance.

Dark eyes searched the darkness of the bridge tonight as though she could find a shred of humanity left in such an arrangement. She felt so very much like a piece of cattle whose prospective owner checked her teeth and poked her ribs before bidding on her.

Her grandmother had taught her better than that. Isabelle still wondered how in the world her mother could have been raised in the same home where she had spent her teen years and become such a different person. At 23, Isabelle had no intention of signing or fulfilling that contract. Not in a million years. And it brought every other agreement into question.

Yes, she had come to the city determined to try. To try to be one of them. A real Atkins girl. She'd let them dye her hair blue and worn the contacts that morphed her eyes from endless brown to an arresting blue. She'd sung the songs that her mother demanded, even when they didn't make her happy.

She'd played the family game of keeping their fans alerted to her every facet of life through tweets and posts on social media. She hardly knew how to fall asleep without an endless parade of her own commentary being reposted and commented on. Her simple existence had morphed into something larger than life and almost too big for her to handle on her own. She'd more than once considered hiring an assistant to manage her online accounts so she could just sneak away and forget about Isabelle Atkins.

Deep inside, she longed for country air and a simpler life.

It was too much. Not only had the fire of her own creative passions been banked and reduced to the latest cookie cutter sound and style, but she was forced to wear her sister's outlandish, eye catching fashions, and she still couldn't outshine her other sister's natural beauty.

Helen literally ran her life, from the times of day she could tweet and what it should say, to the places she could eat and what she could be seen putting in her mouth. Isabelle rarely went anywhere without a swarm of photographers on her tail. And despite the limelight, the constant attention, the social media accounts so full of followers she couldn't blink without someone knowing it, she'd managed this.

This moment on the bridge with no one but her and the phone that was inching further and further over the edge. That brought out a wry smile. Because the girl with the blue hair wasn't just a dumb follower after all. The minute she dropped her look and shed her clothes, she was a wholly different creature, so average without her trappings that no one even noticed her there in the dark of the night.

While visiting her sister's midtown penthouse only a week ago, she'd made the confession. Sunshine streamed through windows that stretched from imported wood floors to ceilings edged in crown molding. Jen was wedged into the couch, no makeup on and a burp cloth over her shoulder. Isabelle was beside her, twisting a lock of blue hair, and weighing her words before she spoke.

"I don't want to do it anymore, Jen," she'd whispered in a rare moment of candor between them. Jen had been cuddling Constellation, who they both dubbed Stella for short, and was entranced by her curls and the utter sweetness of new baby smell.

"What do you mean? The Sportsgirl promo?"

"The Sportsgirl promo, the elite spot in Cosmo, the campaign for Jasper's cologne fragrance. What the heck is Dank anyway? Who wants to spray themselves in Dank?"

"It doesn't mean that anymore, Iz. It means you're in." Jen's platinum blond curls didn't dare tussle when she shook her head. "It's like you're not even trying."

"I'm not, Jenni. I just … I want out."

A gasp caught in Jen's throat, and she sat up almost too quickly, producing a quick little echoing gasp from Stella. Isabelle never used her childhood nickname anymore, and coupled with those words, Jen didn't seem to know what to do with herself. Even looking shocked, she was gorgeous. This week, her hair was platinum blond, her favorite, but she hadn't bothered with contacts yet this morning, so her eyes were their original chocolate brown. Instead of meeting Isabelle's eyes, she focused her gaze on Stella as she laid her onto the couch cushion between them.

"I don't love Jasper."

"Of course you don't! Do you think I loved Colin? I mean, he was hot, I'll give him that, but it was just a matter of connections. The jocks paid attention when I was dating one of them. Sales on our products went through the roof. My online following doubled overnight when we started dating." Jen sipped her morning green smoothie. She never finished it. Ever.

Isabelle studied her fingers, freshly manicured that morning. She'd chosen black for the polish. "Grandma used to say we shouldn't try to be important. We should try to *do* something important with our lives."

Jen looked over at her more startled than before. "This *is* important, Iz. That increase alone meant I could get the Coach bag I've had my eyes on." Isabelle fought the urge to roll her eyes. She still couldn't understand what had happened to her sisters.

"You can't be serious. Jen, after everything with Colin and Stella, you still think this is enough?"

Jen ran a hand through those flawless curls, displacing a few.

"You know what this means, right? The fortune, the cars, the clothes, they'll all be gone. You'd have to get a job, and with our fame, there's no starting over. There's no working your way up like a normal person."

"There is if I disappear." Isabelle's eyes flicked to her sister's face. Her mouth had fallen open in surprise.

"Are you serious?"

Isabelle took her sister's hand. "I've never been more serious. I'm 23. I'm practically betrothed to the town whore with a sentence of five years and two kids. You don't unring that bell, Jen. I want my own life before it's too late."

"Have you told Helen?" It was a whisper. In the moment those words met the air, they divided Isabelle's confidence in two. She needed her sister desperately, but right there, where her words still hung in the air, Isabelle didn't know if she'd done the right thing in trusting her with this confession.

She was banking on the bond they'd always shared to fight its way through, no matter what time and experience had done to change them. Instead of giving in to the doubt sinking in the pit of her stomach, Isabelle feigned confidence in her decision. It wasn't hard. She knew it was the only thing left to do.

"What do you think?" Isabelle shot her a look, one dark eyebrow raised. "Helen would have whisked me off for a quickie wedding in Vegas if she knew anything about it."

Jen laughed, reaching out to scoop up Stella and breathe in her curls again. It was her new habit, a kind of soothing ritual that slowly obliterated the haunting memories of her marriage. She stared out the window of the penthouse for a long moment, seeing nothing but sky while she breathed deep.

"What's your plan?"

Isabelle didn't realize she'd been holding her breath until she let it out in one big puff. This was what she'd been waiting for. The details were already mounting up in her brain, filed under her painstaking research of how to make a clean break.

"I've worked out contract details through a separate attorney who will contact Miller and Tungeman once

I'm gone. He'll also freeze all my accounts—all the ones Helen knows about anyway—until I'm ready to use them under a new name."

Jen's eyes were growing wider with each statement, but she didn't speak.

"A friend of Grandma's has agreed to take me in. I'll have a job, a place to stay—"

"You can't go back to Gunlock, Iz. That's the first place she'll look."

"I'm not," Isabelle assured her.

Jen tapped a finger on her lips as she walked quietly with Stella. "You'll have to leave it all: your phone, your jewelry, anything that defines you as Isabelle Atkins."

Isabelle stared down at the rings on her fingers and started taking them off. "I know." She removed the large loops from her ears and placed them on the table. "My friend will have clothes too. I'll leave all my credit cards, etc. in the care of my attorney. He's working on getting me a new one under a new name. I've worked through all of my current agreements."

"That's why you didn't sign the beach shoot contract last month. Good grief, Iz, you've been planning this for ages."

"I didn't want to leave a mess behind. I wanted to leave with my eyes open."

Jen took her arm—her grasp tight—their eyes locking. Hers were filled with tears. "You really think you can do this? I mean, leave everything, start over? I don't know, Iz. I can already feel the void, and I don't know if I can live without you again."

Isabelle hugged her sister and niece in one fierce squeeze, letting the tears fill her eyes as well. "It won't be forever, Jenni. I couldn't live without you and Stella either. It'll just take a while for the media frenzy to die down."

"I always knew you were stronger than the rest of us," Jen said, her voice hushed by tears. "I knew it from the moment you came home, and your eyes were so bright. You have something inside of you that burns. Just like those fireflies you told me about."

Isabelle grinned. "Fireflies ... I love you, Jen. I always have, and I always will. This life can be whatever you need it to be, you know? You could do or be anything. You don't have to be what Helen says."

Jen drew back, crystal tears glistening on her cheeks. "I was never as strong as you, Iz. But I will be strong this time. I'll help you. I have about ten thousand I can spot you, but it won't last forever."

Isabelle smiled, wiping the tears from her sister's cheek. "You know, some people could live on that for a long time."

Jen smirked. "Yeah, well, they don't have to update their look every week, do they?"

"And neither will I. I just need one last tweak to go under the radar for a while."

A few days later, in a haze of salon odors, Jen turned off the blow drier.

"Wow, I haven't seen you dark since the day you came home."

"Since I was 20." Isabelle smiled at her sister's reflection. Her hair was back to its natural rich brown that matched her eyes. After three years of bright blue, she felt like a different person. Normal. Forgettable. For once, she was grateful for her average looks and build.

Jen hugged her shoulders. "Are you sure you want to do this? I mean, we could just lobby Helen for a different husband contract. There are lots of cute guys who want to date you. Believe me, I've seen the feeds about the subject."

Isabelle shivered. "No thanks. This makes me more sure than ever that this is the right thing to do." She fingered the edge of her dark locks.

Jen looked at their joined reflection for another moment. "I thought you might say that. Here."

She handed Isabelle a pay-by-month cell phone and a small purple coin purse. When she opened it, Isabelle found a wad of bills inside.

"What's this?"

"Let's just say, I made some calls. The phone is untraceable to you. Once you leave, you won't be able to call me on this line." She wiggled her blinged-out phone. "I got my own pay-by-the-month set up and programmed into your phone for emergencies." She held up a pink flip phone. It was such a step down from her diamond encrusted smart phone that they both laughed about it.

"Have you decided on a name?" Jenni asked.

Isabelle clicked the purse shut, sliding both items into the pockets of her plain backpack. "Journey Miller."

"Journey?" Jen nodded, savoring the word on her tongue.

"Remember when Grandma used to say, '*The only journey worth taking is one that leads you to who you're meant to be*'? It just seemed fitting. Far enough from Izzy Atkins to give me a head start in the run of my life."

"I like it. Kind of eighties rockband meets country girl."

The girls hugged, dark hair filtering in amongst blond on their shoulders. "Thanks, Jen."

"Look, Iz. I know this is going to be fun at first and then not. When you get to the hard times, you might feel like giving up, but don't. If you're going to do this, you have to go big or go home. There will be a whole world looking for you, but I'll do my best to point them overseas. You always did love Venice."

Journey swallowed her fear and nodded. "I'm definitely going big. Thank you. I love you."

That was four hours ago.

When the Atkins dynasty allowed napkins to be laid over their laps at a posh restaurant on Fifth and Main, Isabelle had been uncharacteristically absent. Her driver arrived with an empty car, and Jen had no explanation.

"We were together all morning. Everything seemed fine when I left for my pre-dinner massage." Jen was really good at looking innocent.

Isabelle, comfy for the first time in three years in the thrift-store picks leftover from her past, slipped out the fire escape and walked the short distance to the bridge. With a backpack over one shoulder and a black baseball cap pulled down low, she was any girl blending in with the shadows.

The clouds overhead obscured the moon for a long moment, making Isabelle's phone announcements more pronounced than ever. Helen flashed on the screen again in her shouty caps.

> Helen: YOU ARE SO DEAD TO ME RIGHT NOW, YOU SPOILED LITTLE BRAT!!!

A new round of messages sent in quick succession did what one could not. Little by little, the phone reached an imbalance in it's center of gravity, and at last, four inches was not enough to keep it from plunging—screen lit up in a look of cellular surprise—end over end into the rushing water below.

Isabelle Atkins—no, Journey Miller—shifted the backpack over her shoulder and leaned over the bridge railing to watch her phone's bright light be swallowed up in utter darkness. Izzy Atkins was officially off the air.

"You've had three DUIs in the last six months, Cody. What the hell do you expect?"

"Seriously? I pay you six figures to keep me *out* of the courtroom, Ian." Cody Blake slammed his fist into the wall, making the framed diploma shift from perfect center. It did nothing for his broiling temper. His eyes shot to the table of bottles behind the desk. He was dying for just one glass to take the edge off his fury.

"Twelve figures wouldn't get you out of this, man! You're lucky you're not being locked up right now, do you get that?" Ian's normally jovial disposition was jet black, his forehead beaded in sweat and his fists clenched. Cody could tell from the look in his eyes that though they had been best friends for years, at this moment, Ian didn't like anything about him.

Cody turned away from the liquor and shook his head. Ian knew nothing about what he was going through. Man. Couldn't a guy have a good time? Go for a spin in the dark? Why were there so many policemen on his tail anyway? Sounded like a conspiracy for media attention to him. When you're pulling over the hottest country star on the charts, it tells the world you're doing something.

Ian's words filtered through his throbbing head. Probably more of his preaching about doing the right thing and getting clean, but Cody only caught the last words. "So clean up and try to look like you could be redeemable. I think that's about your only hope with this judge."

Hours later, the judge seemed to have the same perspective. It was like he was surrounded by a half dozen people trying to be his dad. The deafening pound of the gavel brought him out of his brood.

The sentence: rehab.

Yeah, like he had a problem. But it was what followed next that got him boiling again. 320 hours of community service. Is he fricken serious?

"To be fulfilled at a location to be determined contingent on your success at the rehab facility appointed," the judge declared. "Mr. Blake, I feel you have a great deal of potential, but you have, like many before you, fallen to the temptations of success. This is your opportunity to get your head back on straight and do something better than waste the life the good Lord gave you. I have certainly seen enough of that today."

"This is a good thing, honey." His mother's soft hand registered on his arm before he shook her off. The fact that she had come all the way from Tennessee for this made his stomach sink. She tried again. "Just think. You'll have so much to write about."

Yeah, right. Like he even sang the songs he wrote. Not if he wanted to hit the charts, he didn't. He'd learned that early in his career. No one wanted to hear heartfelt country anymore. They wanted it mixed in with pop and rap. They wanted tats and dark hats. They wanted edgy, sexy, beat hugging music. That's exactly what he was good at delivering. He knew just how tight to wear his jeans to make the girls scream, and he'd be lying if he said he didn't enjoy the results. He almost grinned at the thought.

The judge's voice brought him back to the present with a jolt.

Community service?

Ugh. What was this, a "Mighty Ducks" movie remake? What did community service mean, anyway? Was he going to be picking up trash on the side of some highway?

His head pounded, a sure sign he wasn't completely through his latest hangover, but lately, one seemed to roll into another. Maybe if he could just get that drink.

Everything the judge said seemed to come out in another language, one his brain was failing to process. He kept looking for the expiration date, the moment he could put this whole embarrassing scene behind him.

"What the hell does this mean?" Cody growled at Ian, barely bothering to keep his voice down. His mother's grip on his arm intensified, and he shook her off, the throb in his head escalating to a teeth gritting scale. He looked frantically around the room for a drink. Anything would do right now. Just *something* to calm him down.

"It means," the judge *had* heard his rude question. He tried to still his shaking hands and focus on the frown lines and white hair making up the judge's face. "Your physician will determine if you've made a full recovery, including a 30-day sobriety test, reinforced by urine testing. In other words, Mr. Blake, you're in for some hard times." When Cody didn't respond, the judge sank back with a grim smile. "Just so you're aware, Mr. Blake, if you find the accommodations at Allen Addiction Recovery too taxing and should desire to make life miserable for those assisting you, your next stop is the state prison facility to serve a sentence to the full extent of the law."

That seemed to have the effect the judge was hoping for. Cody's jaw went slack. His eyes glazed as if he were seeing the word "prison" flash across them in Vegas neon.

"Say yes, sir," Ian urged through the corner of his mouth.

"Yes, sir." Cody repeated, his throat dry. He felt like he might be sick. Stomach churning, he turned to his mom again.

"We're praying for you, Cody." She murmured into his chest as she gripped him to her.

Pesky flies diving around his head, that's what those words felt like. Could this day get any worse? Maybe if he could just get home, he could have a beer and relax before facing this new challenge. He needed to call Tiffany and his agent and get things settled before he went in for this ridiculous exercise.

Maybe, when his head stopped pulsing, Ian and he could figure a way out of this. He certainly didn't need a rehab facility. Inpatient was a bit excessive for a spin around town after a few drinks. This judge was clearly biased.

"Please empty your pockets, sir." The deep voice of a court officer cut off his train of thought. Cody turned to see him holding open a see-through personal effects bag.

"What?" Cody felt the blood drain from his face. He must be hallucinating. That had happened once before.

"They're taking you to Allen now, Cody," Ian said, swallowing. He couldn't meet Cody's eyes.

"They're what?" Cody's voice was rising. Panic squeezed his insides. This had to be a mistake. He whirled, but the judge was already gone. His mother's soothing voice didn't even register over the fury boiling up inside him.

"Your sentence at Allen Addiction Recovery begins right now, Mr. Blake. You can leave your personal effects with your next of kin, your legal representation, or put them in this bag where they will be sealed and kept by the state until the time you're released from custody."

Cody turned on Ian. "I'm being taken into custody right now? Are you in on this too?"

He sounded hysterical even to himself, but control was just outside the reach of his trembling fingertips.

"Cody, don't do this. There are photographers …" Ian leaned in, but it wasn't a good idea. Cody's control slipped even further, and the next thing he knew, his fist was meeting the nose of his attorney. He felt his arms being restrained and saw the spatter of blood on his best friend's white suit shirt. He recognized the damning look in Ian's eye, a look that said he didn't even know him anymore. His mother's quiet sobs in the background became a nonstop earworm, punctuated by the clicking sound of cuffs tightening around his wrists.

To ice it all, the next click he heard was a whir of high-powered camera lenses, shuttering repeatedly. His life was over.

Chapter Two

"Humans are vile," Journey gasped, pressing her back against the wall outside the men's bathroom. Her hair, once neatly coifed every single day by a professional stylist, was now hidden beneath an orange bandanna that clashed with her skin tone and made her wish she had never seen a urinal in all her days.

Ruby's head popped up from behind the kitchen counter, her strawberry blond hair in twin pigtails—this week tipped in violet. "Ya know, I always used to have this strange fascination with the boy's bathroom, like … what was going on in there? Why weren't we allowed to use it when the girls' gets backed up? That kind of thing."

She leaned on the counter with her chin in her hands. "So once, I snuck in with my friend, Suzi Baker. She created a diversion by fainting. She could do it like that! One exposure and that crazy fascination was squelched like a kiwi under a pair of size tens. One peek at a urinal pretty much does it for you. Man, looks like you could use one of these."

Journey's brows did what they always did when Ruby started on one of her crazy stories, rising to the top of her forehead in expectant waiting. She never knew where it would end up, so she just went with it, a curious smile on her lips. In the end there would be treats, and most likely, something else to laugh about.

Ruby was unlike anyone Journey had ever met. Finished with her tale, Ruby slid an oven-baked confection over to Journey's side of the counter. Journey eyed the treat for a moment, battling her inner red-carpet critic.

"It looks like it has chocolate in it."

"You like chocolate." Ruby's smile was encouraging.

"I know. But after last time ..." She didn't want to dredge up the fact that she'd been unable to stop at one or two of Ruby's last tasty treats. She'd forced herself from the room after stuffing four in her face.

"This has mind altering capabilities, so if we're being logical, this could be seen as more of a psychological treatment than a dessert." That smile again. Bright, effusive, and almost totally impossible to resist when coupled with chocolate-laced treats.

Journey couldn't help but return it. Pushing off from the wall, she washed her hands—twice—then picked up the little square. One tentative bite and she had forgotten the aim problems of the entire male species.

"Rubes, this has to be illegal!"

Ruby's smile went from watchful to beaming in half a second flat. She clapped her hands. "Right? Cheesecake brownies. I'm putting them on the menu. On weekends only, of course."

"Of course," Journey smirked, "because you're also a tease."

"You know me so well, Journey girl. And I know you well enough to know you're going to want to hug me and scream after the next piece of news I have for you."

Journey was buried in her brownie and didn't fully register this, so Ruby waited, her plump arms folded over her white chef coat.

"Hmm … what?" Journey looked up, running her tongue over her teeth to gather up any more delightful fragments.

"Good news? Hug and scream?"

Journey stopped long enough to examine her new best friend. She had come to Snowflake Falls Inn with nothing but hope, determination, and a name that had to be called at least twice before she remembered it was hers. For the last three months, she'd tucked away the ten thousand dollars her sister sent her with and revisited what it felt like to live like an average human being.

Turns out—in the real world—no one woke her up for her morning massage.

There was no personal trainer.

If there was anywhere to drive, she would have to do it herself.

The down-to-earth reality of it felt a lot like her life before moving back to the city. It felt like home, and

Grandma, and everything that had been good in her life since she turned twelve.

She loved the inn, from it's rugged location tucked up against the rocks of the mountain, to it's three stories of well appointed rooms. Just off the entry with it's tall registration desk was a spacious gathering room with various collections of comfortable seating. This adjoined a dining area with a counter lined by barstools where one could nibble Ruby's latest culinary brilliance.

Out behind the main building were five little cabins, and Journey had taken up residence in cabin four. She loved that the inn was run by Mama Lucille and Big Ben, as they insisted they be called.

Big Ben was a tower of a man with large hands and a substantial beard. Despite his formidable appearance, he had a ready smile and a lively sense of humor.

Lucille was his perfect compliment. Though she was a bit more introspective than her husband, Mama had become just as much of an ally from the moment Journey set foot in the inn. The easy comfort and slow pace of the inn reminded her of her grandma's home. So many things did.

Except for her job on the cleaning crew. There were things—even with living on a small farm—that Journey had never had to do. Cleaning boys' bathrooms was one of them, and to be honest, the ladies' version wasn't so hot either.

Journey came into it knowing she'd have to work hard. She realized she'd have to be disciplined. She guessed she might be lonely.

It was all true, times ten.

The hailstorm of media attention, blasted on the flat screen, had settled into an occasional teaser about sightings of Isabelle Atkins all over the world. Journey missed her sister. She missed Stella. She even missed some of the perks of being a part of the Atkins team.

In the midst of that loneliness, a bright light illuminated the darkness. Her name was Ruby Whitaker. Friendly, vivacious, and *so* unlike any of the girls Journey had spent time with in the last three years of her life, Ruby was full figured and self-confident.

Of course, as a girl who had eaten less in the last three years than she had in the one year before moving to the city, Journey noticed both those characteristics with great interest. Ruby loved every part of her curvy, cheerful self. She loved food—tasting it, making it, sharing it. She also loved nature and life and laughing.

Ruby saw Journey walk in with a bandanna around her short dark hair after her first time washing up a bathroom, and there she was. A ray of shining light, holding out a cinnamon roll the size of Journey's head. There's something about being rescued with a plate of cinnamon and sugar that bonds one for life. Now, Journey couldn't imagine a world that didn't include Ruby.

Presently, Ruby's face was alight with the news she was holding in.

"Okay, spill it, Rubes. I can't handle much after that brownie. I'm going into sugar shock already."

"Lucille mentioned wanting to see you once you were done with your shift. I think she has an opening that will take you out of bathroom duty and into the light!" She talked like that. In poetry and big movements, her white chef shirt waving around with her arms.

She was eight parts genius and two parts absent-minded. She could be deboning a chicken one moment and then waving her knife at you in serious conversation the next. And the best part was that during Journey's gloom of loneliness, Ruby made her laugh. Like now, when she was literally bouncing up on the tips of her toes in anticipation. Journey was short, and Ruby was only an inch or two taller.

"Lucille probably just wants to be sure I got that mysterious gunk out of room five."

"Well, go on and find out. I'll just be waiting here, making something amazing for dinner. So, get. I can't wait anymore. I've been holding on to that secret since this morning."

Journey shrugged, rolling her mop bucket out the back door. She went through the ritual of emptying and stowing the cleaning supplies and washed her hands two—no, better make it three—more times. Journey crossed through the dining room and continued past the large gathering room dominated by a substantial stone fireplace. Overstuffed chairs and comfy sofas were arranged throughout the space to make for easy conversation. She'd passed many a day off curled up with a book in one of those chairs. It was her favorite thing to do when she wasn't soaking up the sunshine, dipping her toes in the ice cold lake or exploring the trails that crisscrossed the mountainside.

Hurrying through the entry and past the registration desk, Journey turned down the hall to an office where Lucille would be waiting. The door was slightly ajar, and Journey heard Lucille's strong voice finishing up a phone call.

"It is not going to be a problem, Ian. In my opinion, everyone deserves a chance to change their lives. God has been good enough to grant me more than one. Leave it to me."

Journey shrank back, not wanting to intrude on a personal call, but the shift in her position must have caught Lucille's eye, because she replaced the phone and called out to her.

"Come in, Journey." Mama Lucille was an old friend of her grandma's and an exceptional woman. They'd connected at Grandma's funeral before Journey left for the city. Her words then had been, "Your grandmother was my dear friend. There will come a time in the next few years when you're going to need some help. I'm here to give it."

With those few words came an exchange of numbers and, for Journey, a complete forgetting of the incident until three months ago when she knew she was going to be breaking ties with everything that constituted her world. Out of nowhere, Lucille's name came to her mind with force, and somehow, when she called and told her what was happening and what she needed, Lucille was more than happy to offer her a place and a job until she was ready to move on.

Lucille felt like a hug after a rough day and a cheering squad when she was pretty sure she had as much hope for success as the male praying mantis. Where Grandma June had been salt and pepper hair and brown eyes, Lucille's hair was a gently faded red and her eyes a crystal blue.

"Ruby said you might want—"

"Oh, yes. I have been hoping you would come by. I've got a proposition for you, Journey. Now, I'm going to be forthright with you about this." She paused, waiting for Journey to sit and chew on that word. Who says forthright these days? It was just one more thing Journey liked about her.

"Okay. I'm ready."

Lucille turned a smile on her that was sunshine on a cold wet day. She never tired of the warmth.

"There's a young man coming to the inn to do some community service after a prolonged stay in rehab. He's been quite a mess, Journey, but he's much closer to being on track than off, and I'm happy to give him this opportunity to serve his time constructively. Because of his popularity, completing his sentence in the city would be a bit ... distracting. Do you understand?"

Journey nodded thoughtfully. She could easily imagine. Some political bad boy rehabbing it and serving CS would get a lot of press attention. The summers at Snowflake Falls tended to be a bit low key, mostly weddings, anniversary celebrations and group getaways. But what would he do?

"You know we've had Adam helping with our day tours, right? Quads, hiking, swimming, canoeing?"

"Sure." Journey nodded. She'd kept to herself for the most part, but she wasn't blind. Adam was totally handsome yet also totally married.

"Well, he got accepted at the university for the summer term, and he will be starting next week. Ben and I could use some help with the tours in his absence. After some thought, we agreed that this young man could work out his community service leading the daily excursions. He's obviously a social person. We think he could do well, and it would help us tremendously."

Journey cocked her head to the side, putting the pieces together. "Only, he needs a babysitter?"

Lucille's smile widened. "Ben and I would like to offer you a position as co-captain of the daily tours. We are running a business after all, and we need to know he is on his best behavior with our guests. Mind you, his sobriety and behavior has nothing to do with your pay. You're not in charge of keeping him clean. You're just there to lend a hand, make our guests happy, and report if things get hairy."

Journey sat back, folding her arms over her chest and considering the offer. "Report?"

Lucille leaned forward, weaving her long slender fingers together on the desktop. "I'm not asking you to be a tattle-tale, Journey. But if this guy is intent on returning to his old ways, I can't let him harm our reputation or our guests."

Journey's head bobbed in understanding.

"Your pay would increase, and the best part yet: no more toilets." Lucille chuckled heartily. "Though, I don't think I've ever had a more dedicated sanitizer."

"You should have started with that," Journey laughed. "When do I start?"

"Our refugee gets here tomorrow morning. We'll meet at lunch when the biggest crowds are out exploring and get things hammered out."

Journey left the office with a smile lit by nuclear power on her face. In the kitchen, Ruby paused, her pastry bag of cream puff filling poised in midair.

"What did she say?" Ruby was breathless.

"No more toilets for me!" Journey crowed. That's when Ruby's prophecy of squealing and hugging came true—with a side of cream puff filling.

ೞ❄❄❄ೞ

Cody's first glance at Snowflake Falls Inn felt like a repeat of a horror novel. Birds singing. Sunshine bursting through the trees. Freaking, fresh mountain air. Any moment he expected a chainsaw wielding madman to come blazing through the trees to end his miserable life in a bloody assault.

He stared out the window of Ian's SUV, his teeth clenched. It wasn't bad enough that he had been in rehab for an extra month, now he was stuck at some nowhere inn on some remote mountain for another two months of community service. *Two months!* This nightmare seemed never-ending. His summer tour had been canceled, his fans refunded. His agent was working to reschedule everything for the fall. Every blow felt so close to fatal for him and his career.

Cody had come pretty far, if he was being fair. After a miserable, wasted month of being a complete ass to everyone at Allen, it was a miracle he hadn't spent more than a week in prison before swallowing his pride enough to ask for another chance.

He'd jumped through the hoops, talked about his childhood (nothing to tell) and his tumble into drinking—okay, into alcoholism—and had come to realize that the people who had been surrounding him lately, telling him the things he wanted to hear, weren't exactly the kind of people who were watching out for his well-being. They were more than happy to see him tank himself and reap the benefits of the tabloid press.

The only people who'd stuck next to him through the whole of it were Ian and his mother. A woman he still had a hard time thinking of without a great deal of self-loathing. He couldn't believe he'd put his sweet mom through this kind of misery. Ruining his own life sucked, but seeing his mother suffer was another thing entirely.

That didn't make this transition any easier. What he wanted to do was get back to his life. Find out why Tiffany, his girlfriend of seven months, wasn't returning his calls. Why, he had been gone for three months and she'd never once picked up her cell when he'd tried to call her or even tried calling him. He couldn't believe she would just drop him for something like this.

"Cody …"

"Yeah?" Cody wrenched his mind back to the present and off his girlfriend.

"I take it you weren't listening to that whole thing."

Cody shrugged. "You know I don't want to be here, man."

"It's this or finish out your time in a jail cell. I take it you weren't a fan." Ian wasn't pulling any punches. They'd gotten past the bloody nose Cody had left him with in the courtroom, but Ian had a different edge to him since Cody's rehab. People had changed a lot … or maybe it was him.

"Yeah, not the highlight of my life." There was an edge to his voice, his jaw clenched. Ian watched him for a moment and then led out a pent-up breath.

"Look, I know this is hard. But this is your *life*, man. *Nothing*—not the music, not the money, not the girls—nothing is worth more than getting your life back on track. Or, it shouldn't be. So, you've got to spend some time giving back and practicing the sober lifestyle. So, what? Could you ask for a better backdrop? I mean, come on. It's better than a poke in the eye with a dirty stick. This place is beautiful. You'll be outdoors, back to your roots. Something good has to come from the time you spend here."

Cody glared at the surroundings, refusing to notice the burst of sunshine filtering through the pine needles, the grace of mountain air filling his nostrils, or the sound of water flowing nearby. He refused to be moved by it, and he didn't know why. Finally, he blurted the question that had been broiling inside of him for the last few months.

"I just want to know what happened to Tiff. Three months. Don't I even get to see her before all this starts?"

Ian looked away, but Cody caught the expression in his eyes before he did. The look of pity that he despised.

"What? Is she gone? Seriously? Seven months and now this?"

"Cody, dude. You knew she was only into you for the money and booze. She showed up for the party."

Cody clenched his fist, resisting the urge to plow it into Ian's face again. It wasn't his fault that the words he said were true enough to pierce deep and sharp.

"How long?"

Ian didn't meet his gaze for a long time. "What does it matter?"

"How long, Ian?"

Ian shook his head, raking a hand through blond hair. He finally met Cody's gaze with his own frank one. "From day one, dude. She bailed on day one and found herself a new boy-toy to follow around. Cody, you're better off, man. She wasn't any good for you. Do you think a woman like that is going to be the one?"

"I wasn't looking for the one," Cody grumbled, lighting streaking his already gray-sky mood. "I was only looking for a good time, anyway."

"Yeah, well, about that. You know the stipulations the owners put on the next two months. I know you don't want your best friend drilling them into you, but as your attorney, I am under obligation to list them out for you so I can say I've done my due diligence. No messing around with the girls. No drinking, smoking, drugs, etc. Urine sample weekly. You're to report to Ben for that sample. Barring any relapses or general bad behavior, you get your life back in eight weeks. Until then, your time belongs to Ben and Lucille, owners of Snowflake Falls Inn."

"So, I'm basically in hell."

"Basically. Only this hell is on a freaking mountainside with all the amenities. But yeah, whatever."

Cody rolled his eyes. "Fine. Let's get this over with."

※ ❋ ❋ ❋ ※

Journey was curled up in an overstuffed chair in the gathering room set before the enormous main fireplace. She was absorbed in a brand-new novel she'd been dying to read, soaking up the pages and the bliss of her change in position. Distressed jeans and a butter-soft T-shirt under a zip-up hoodie the color of warm salmon cocooned her into a happy spot she knew she would soon need to abandon. The meeting was moments away, but this was one of those books she just couldn't put down. The dark-haired heroine and a hunky basketball-playing hero were moments away from their long awaited first kiss. She was a total sucker for happily-ever-afters.

Off in the kitchen, she could hear Ruby humming something while pans clattered, and the inevitable something fell to the ground followed by a short string of pseudo curses. Ruby was too sunny to rely on four letter words for her exclamations. Instead, Journey overheard strings of, "*Son of a biscuit baker!*" or, "*Holy crackers!*" The grin that turned up her cheeks at her friend's squeaky-clean tirades was impossible to suppress.

The brightness of Ruby's disposition kicked open the door of memories for Journey.

Grandma.

Bright sunshine.

White washed walls and mason jars of flowers.

Peonies. Roses. Delphiniums.

Their hue and scent colored her remembrances of home. Home. A home that was long gone now. Easily disposed of and sold off in a matter of weeks once a headstone was all that remained of her beloved grandmother.

Rolling her shoulders, she refocused on her book and flicked lint off the pillow under her arm. She read a few words before her mind wandered again to one of her favorite memories.

Grandma June loved to hear her sing. She was the one who insisted on the guitar lessons. She was the one who called her onto the back porch when the fireflies were out and let her serenade them to sleep. Making music was breathing and laughter in Grandma's house.

This night she came home devastated by a boy, of course. The boy she'd been hoping was into her most definitely was not. And that meant the world was ending.

She could still hear Grandma's voice, like a rub of velvet over her skin. "Sweet girl, you're not the first one who's known this heartbreak. You most certainly won't be the last." A gentle rub of her fingertips over Journey's dark hair, and then, she scooped her face into her hands and gazed into her eyes. They were the same. Dark and deep and full of words that hadn't been spoken.

"Bella, this life isn't about enduring the downs. You've got a gift. All of us get them, but not many of us find them so well at your age. When you hurt like this, there's time for tears. And then there's time to use your gift to change the world, to make it a little better … or maybe to just make *you* better."

"Singing isn't going to help, Grandma." There was a lot of pathetic snot involved in that statement.

Grandma hummed a little and laughed. "Well, it might not. It might not."

She never argued; she just loved. She slipped an arm around Journey's shoulder, letting her wallow in her misery for several long moments. Journey listed out her faults.

She wasn't pretty enough.

Her hair was too frizzy.

Her thighs touched.

In spite of herself, the lyrics started writing themselves in her head. A tune dared to join them. She tried not to hum along, but it was really good. Without thinking, she found herself mumbling a few of the words along with the music in her head and then pressed her lips together.

Grandma just smiled, and Journey knew she couldn't handle it anymore. She'd learned quickly that words had to be captured while they were living, or she'd miss the best ones.

"Grandma, I have to go."

"Okay," Grandma said, not asking questions. Later that night, she brought out her guitar and perched on the edge of the old sofa in the living room. She sang it all to Grandma. Her final line had Grandma tipping her head back in laughter, her brown eyes shining with delight.

"It's not about my thighs, after all.

I don't think I like you anymore."

Grandma laughed and then cheered. "Sing it again, girl. That right there is therapy for the broken-hearted."

The front door chimed, and someone cursed, making Journey sit up and come back from her memory. Ironically, the sound of the voice from the doorway jettisoned Journey into another memory, one that left her feeling more like a slug just crawled over her grave, as Grandma would say, than warm and fuzzy.

In an instant, Journey could recall the night she heard a voice much like that, live and in the flesh. She was still Isabelle Atkins, in all her blue haired glory, appearing on an awards show. He was the reason country music couldn't have nice things. Tall, admittedly handsome, but horribly arrogant, Cody Blake made Isabelle want to throw a punch. That was saying something, because while she had her spiteful moments, she wasn't usually violent.

Journey shook her head to wash out the recollection and the bad taste lingering on her tongue while her fingers slid a bookmark in between pages and tucked the volume into the side of the chair as she stood.

She caught sight of Ruby standing at the kitchen serving counter, her rubber spatula frozen in midair, a large glop of whipping cream slowly easing toward the handle under the power of gravity. Her mouth gaped ever so slightly while her eyes went starry. Everyone had been briefed on the high profile guy coming in for community service.

Curious, Journey rounded the corner just as Mama Lucille's voice filled the room. She would have remained unnoticed if she hadn't let out a puff of shocked air that drew everyone's attention.

Journey was thinking in curse words.

There was reason that slimy slug of a memory had come up.

Cody Blake was standing at the registration counter.

Chapter Three

This was definitely not how she envisioned her first day off of toilet duty. She was standing behind the wall that led to the gathering room. Ruby's eyebrow was raised in her direction while she swiped up a glop of whipped cream and went back to work on the project in front of her.

Lucille showed the men at the counter into the gathering room while Journey worked on fixing her face. Right now, it was stuck on I-hate-you-for-breathing mode. Closing her eyes, she took a deep breath, rummaged around for a picture of Grandma in her mind, and smiled. There. That was where she needed to keep it. Cody Blake could *not* know that she, Isabelle Atkins, was holed up at Snowflake Falls Inn. Not after going three months without even so much as a sighting in the entire state. This couldn't be as bad as she thought. There had to be some rational reason why Fate would allow the likes of Blake to cross the hallowed threshold of her sanctuary.

Journey hurried back to her chair, her smile feeling a little false by the time Lucille walked in, followed by a blonde man in a suit and Cody. He didn't look her way, which gave her plenty of time to stare. And yes, there was reason to do so. The last time she saw him, he was in his ridiculous glory. Cowboy hat. Tight jeans. A screen-print T with the title of his latest hit song graphically imposed on it. His dark hair had been styled in impeccable waves. Today, she met a different man. His posture was slumped, and though he was smartly dressed, his hair was too long, his beard overgrown, and his gaze grave. His overall persona said, "Life sucks," on every level.

Battening down her smile, she joined Lucille as Ben walked in and shook hands.

"Ian, Cody, this is my wife, Lucille. This is one of our new summer employees, Journey, and—"

Ruby entered the room, her violet tipped hair in matching pig tails again, her smile buoyant enough for everyone in the room to use as a life preserver, and her hands full of delicious lemon bread under a light drizzle of citrus glaze.

"This is Ruby, our amazing cook."

"Would you like a slice? I'm a *huge* fan!"

Journey rolled her eyes and grabbed the plate that was listing to one side in a quick move, rescuing the bread that was slowly edging toward the ground. "Why don't you grab some plates, Ruby? I'll cut this."

Both men nodded through each introduction. Journey ducked her head when she felt Cody's gaze linger over her for a fraction longer than necessary.

They all settled into overstuffed chairs and sofas.

The suit-wearing Ian was talking now. At least he had some manners. And intelligence. Journey liked him at once despite his connection to Cody.

Cody hadn't looked up since falling into the couch. He seemed mesmerized by the lines of the wood floor until Ruby hurried back into the room with a stack of tiny white plates she carefully placed on the table. Journey served up slices of bread, and Ruby handed them around, positively bursting with swoony delight each time her eyes met Journey's. Without even speaking, Journey could see that she was spazzing out. Her face said things like:

Is it really him?

Oh, gosh, he's gorgeous!

Do you think he would think it was weird if I sat next to him?

I wouldn't do that.

Do you think?

Journey was glad she was only thinking it, not saying it. When she was done passing out bread, they both took a plate and sat together on the couch to the left of the visitors. Journey did her best to hide behind Ruby and generally fade into the wallpaper while keeping her friend out of trouble.

It was all Journey could do to remember not to pull out her phone, snap a picture, and start an online battle. Thank goodness all her accounts had been deleted, and she couldn't even access a signal long enough to make any kind of statement. Oh, and her phone was Stone Age.

"Thank you, ladies," Lucille said, signaling a beginning to the meeting. As everyone enjoyed their treat, Lucille continued, turning her attention to Cody. "Mr. Bainfroth here sent the paperwork over this morning, and Ben and I have reviewed and signed it. I think all that's left is for you to agree to the terms and sign for yourself."

Cody looked like he wanted to say something, and Journey sat back, her eyes leveling on him like laser beams all too willing to flay him apart.

Instead, Lucille continued. "But before we get to all the official business, I want you to know you're welcome here. As a young man trying to make restitution, and as a friend. We've all been down a road we weren't proud of, but not everyone makes the choice to come back.

"Now, I've read all the reports, gotten the facts from Mr. Bainfroth, and considered all the options. In my mind, this place is about as good as it gets when it comes to community service. You've got a right nice place to sleep, food sent from heaven by Miss Ruby here, and your companion will be one of my hardest workers, Miss Journey. You can do a lot of good, or you can be miserable, that choice is yours. But we're happy you're here and glad to be a part of changing your life."

Cody looked at Ian with a pained expression. The truth was, it was hard to bull crap around Lucille. She was a woman who saw through a façade and didn't care one bit about the way you made your money or how much you normally raked in. What she saw was the person, pure and simple. And man, was it a tough gaze to endure when one wasn't exactly happy about who they were.

Ian leaned forward, his face earnest. "We can't thank you and Ben enough, Mama Lucille. We've talked about how great this situation is."

"But he's not buying it." There you go. Lucille cutting to the chase.

"I *like* who I am," Cody grumbled. "So I'm not looking to change my life. I'm just trying to get this behind me and move on. I have concert dates and appearances to make up. I have a fricken photo shoot with AMC magazine that's on hold while I go through this whole … *thing*. It's been three months, and I'm more than anxious to get this over with."

"Eager, that's a beginning." Lucille winked at Journey, and she did her best to retrieve that smile she'd been holding on to. The thing was, his attitude made her blood boil. He didn't see what a huge stroke of good luck he'd just run into by getting connected with Ben and Lucille and the inn. He was just biding his time until he could bolt back to his old life and ways. It was infuriating.

Ben cleared his throat. "We're not asking you to be anyone you're not, Cody. We do need someone who can work hard and be responsible for the guests at our inn. Ian may have told you, but you'll be leading out on the daily excursions around the mountain. Journey, here, will show you around tonight so you can get a feel for the trails. We have ATVs, lakes, canoes, and hiking.

Journey will be your partner, and you'll confer with her on a daily basis. I'll be the one you check in with for your weekly business with the court."

"Tour guide?"

The words, shot at Ian from the side of his mouth, had bite to them. Obviously, Mr. Country Superstar felt this was beneath him.

Mr. Bainfroth turned to look at his client and his face said everything:

Get it together.

Don't blow this.

You're a flippin' idiot.

"Sounds great." Ian turned back with a strained smile.

"Seems to me like you've done a piece of hard work in your life, before the fancy photo shoots, Mr. Blake." Ben stroked his beard for a moment and then continued. "I'd venture a guess that this arrangement might be easier to handle than some of the other options."

"It may not seem like it," Ian said, "but Mr. Blake is so appreciative of this opportunity. There aren't many places he can go unnoticed."

"Keep up the mountain-man look, and he should do okay," Journey said, and then realized she'd spoken aloud. She offered that smile again to make it sound like she was joking, but she needn't have worried. Ben and Lucille both smiled right back.

"She might be on to something there. I'd keep the beard and do your best to resist the urge to flirt with all the ladies." Big Ben leveled a gaze at him. "That's in keepin' with your probation terms as well."

"Yeah," Cody grumbled, "I've been reminded of that repeatedly."

Journey shot Ruby a commiserating look only to find her near swoon. Instead of hearing snarky comments, she was just hearing Cody's dreamy, deep voice. Journey rolled her eyes and turned back to the conversation.

"Let's finish up the paperwork," Lucille suggested, "and Journey, you pull around the Ranger. You can help these gentlemen get Mr. Blake's things to Cabin 5 and then take Mr. Blake out for a little overview of the trails."

"Great," Journey and Cody grumbled in unison. Ian chuckled under his breath, and Ruby sighed. This was going to be a long summer.

෨✼✼✼ඐ

Journey settled behind the wheel of the four-seater, off-road vehicle. She took them up the trails past the tidy row of cabins. Each one had an ample front porch lined in twinkle lights that glowed welcomingly in the deep dark of a mountain night. After waiting for Cody to unload his suitcases, guitar, and mental baggage, she'd left him to stow his crazy while she grabbed a sweater from her cabin.

Now she was trying to get a handle on her nerves. At this point, she wasn't worried about him knowing who she was. The man barely looked at her. He was too busy soaking in his self-loathing and general discontent. He was miserable from head to foot, even in his flashy city clothes. She took a deep breath to still the worry that had bubbled in her stomach since he'd first walked into the inn. She knew it was a bad idea, but she tried striking up conversation nevertheless.

"Have you ever run one of these before?"

"A lot better than you're running it," Cody mumbled under his breath.

Another deep breath kept her from burning him with an equally scathing retort. Instead, she shot him a dark look, her brown eyes boiling with fire that she hoped he could feel despite the cool of the trees they were driving through.

"Wonderful, a total jerk, too. Look, I know you're some kind of big-shot country singer, but obviously, your life plan has tanked. I'd suggest trying the sippy cup of humility Karma has handed you, or you'll end up getting it through a fire hose. As for me, I'm not doing this to stroke your ego or make you feel like a rockstar. Plan on getting your hands dirty and reign in the bad attitude. Lucille may be all about nurturing your inner growth, but I bite."

She wrenched the wheel and Cody cursed under his breath as they jostled over some tree roots followed by a bed of gravel and back onto the trail on the other side.

"Just try not to kill us on our first outing, `kay?" Cody bit out.

Journey's dark eyes could have been registered as murder weapons. "Your wish is my command."

Just ahead, the trees broke open to a meadow filled with flowers interspersed by pockets of thick mud. Rain from the day before mixed with general wet conditions to set up the perfect payback: an enormous mud puddle, so black it looked like wet cow manure. Too bad it was just rich mountain soil. Aiming the Ranger just right, she changed course and gunned the engine. Cody noticed the looming mud just in time, his escalating string of, "Nononononoooooooo!" music to her ears.

The large tires on the Ranger took to the mud like a toddler to cotton candy. They dove in, the tires spinning and spitting mud in all directions. Journey felt a cool splatter across her forehead. Her left arm went black, her leg from thigh to ankle taking the brunt. She had to pull over and wipe off the splats that had blackened her sunglasses.

Oh, but the cherry on top was when she turned to see Cody. Laughter bubbled up before she could check herself. Oh, my. That had worked even better than she'd hoped. When their eyes met, she could tell he was ready to up his sentence from DUI to manslaughter.

Dark, thick mud, the exact hue of wet tar, had flung itself across his face, obscuring his sunglasses almost completely.

Those fancy butt-hugging jeans he'd worn? Black.

The light blue button up that matched his eyes and hugged his rugged chest? *Black.*

His neck, ears, scraggly beard ... everything? *Black*, black, *black*.

"You think this is funny?" He was shouting, spitting mud from his teeth, scraping it off his face, flinging it to the ground in ever-growing disgust, and looking over his clothes like he was on the verge of a toddler meltdown.

"You should see yourself." Journey's giggles were uncontrollable as she grabbed her phone and snapped a pic to show Ruby. Even this Stone-Age flip phone had a little camera, and today she was grateful. He had stepped out of the Ranger and was scraping the muck from his chest. It was a good look for him, actually. The dark sludge plastered itself to every muscle and curve, accentuating his already manly physique. Had he wanted to, he could really fit in as a country boy instead of the ridiculous bad boy he tried to play.

"This outfit was $565.00," he raged, holding the shirt out from his chest and breaking the lovely suction he had going for him. "I bought it *yesterday*."

"And?" She resisted the urge to shoot video and post it to YouTube. *Why* did she have to give up national humiliation as a hobby just before this moment? She even had a title picked out: "Country Music Pretty Boy goes POSTAL in the Middle of Nowhere."

"And it's ruined. This isn't going to come out." He turned bright blue eyes on her and she couldn't help the flirtatious smile that burst out of her.

"You poor thing." She tried to look sympathetic, but knew her frown was more impish than compassionate. "I know it must be hard to think of replacing that stunning outfit with thrift store pickings, but somehow, the little people of the world make do."

He seemed equally stunned by her smile because his rage tamped down for a moment. However, her sassy words made him rally.

"You think I'm a total pretty-boy prick, I get it. Loud and clear." He emphasized each word with his fury.

"Good." She stood up in the Ranger and walked toward him across the front seat, bringing herself to his eye level. "Because I didn't sign up for your bad attitude. Mama Lucille and Big Ben are the best people I know. If you think I'm going to let you be a complete jerk to their guests or make their lives miserable in *any way* when they're just trying to keep your sorry butt out of jail, then you've got something else coming. I will make your life a living hell if you mess with them." She spread out her hands to encompass the mess of the puddle plow they'd experienced. "*This* is just a taste of the misery to come."

He crossed his arms over his chest, the look on his face hovering between humor and disgust. He was watching her during her speech, his eyes moving up and down her small frame. "I'm supposed to be afraid of a deranged tree sprite who can't drive a Ranger to save her life?"

That did it. Journey jumped down, letting her boots splash more mud onto his expensive shoes. She may not look threatening, but she had her ways, and she was going to make sure he took her seriously.

"This isn't about me. It's about my friends." Her voice was dangerous.

He barked a harsh laugh, glaring down at her. "Oh, yeah? From my experience, friends come and go. These people may be your friends now, but they'll turn on you the minute things go bad."

Journey pushed out an annoyed breath. This guy was a mess. "You don't know what friends are then, Cody Blake. And I'd feel sorry for you if I gave a crap about your spoiled, selfish life. You've never met two more loyal people. If Lucille says you're one of us, then you are. As for me, I don't like people so easily, so it won't bother me one bit to do this."

Chapter Four

His arms were still crossed, and he was too distracted by the fact that she was getting close to him and looking amazingly good with black mud splattered across her pretty face. He didn't notice how near he was to the edge of the mud, or how it sank down several inches at the rim. He didn't notice until she rushed up and shoved, harder than he would have imagined her little frame could handle. With nothing to reach for, he went flying. Back into the cold, slimey puddle. There was a sickening squish as anything that may have been clean succumbed to total immersion. For one surprised instant, he looked like a kid making a mud angel.

At this point, he had nothing to lose. He reacted more on the instinct of a kid with three older brothers than an adult with arguably rusty social skills. If he was going down, he was going to walk out with a good story, one that didn't end with him being pushed into the mud by a girl. Before she realized his plan, he had her over his shoulder.

"Don't you dare!" she gasped, but she was laughing too, and before he knew it, they were both in the middle of that mud pit. He plopped her into it, but she didn't fall in full-bodied like he had. She made it look way better, the mire clinging to the figure he'd forgotten to notice, and making it more appealing than he liked. Within seconds, she was up, a glop of sludge in her hand. She didn't waste time flinging it.

There was an audible splat when it hit his cheek and a cool wet sensation as it slithered down his face and mingled into his beard.

"You did not just do that."

A second splat told him she was not waiting for his approval or playing by any rules. The fight was on, and man, was she scrappy. He had to be on his game to make good on his aim. He could say one good thing about being alcohol free for three months. His senses were sharp, and his Little League training came in handy.

Soon, she was almost as covered as he was. He rushed over, scooping up mud as he did. With one hand he grabbed her fist full of muck just before she slung it and twisted her up against his chest. His hand of mud was suspended over her head, ready to trickle down into her hair. She wriggled, but this was where his muscular build had an advantage. He didn't underestimate her strength like he had before.

"Call a truce." He ordered.

"Don't *tell* me what to do." She emphasized the 'tell' with an elbow to the ribs. He groaned but didn't loosen his grip.

"Call a truce, *please*," he amended, completely shocked when the word left his mouth. His mother would be appalled at how seldom he'd used it in the last three years.

"Fine. Truce. Now get off me." Something about her small frame made him want to hold her tight, but he let go, watching her spin out of reach, her hands finding her hips, her deep brown eyes just as feisty as before.

Oh, they were such a serious mess. Her dark ponytail was covered with matching mud. He was filthy from top to bottom. The shoes he'd hoped to salvage squished with every move. And yet, there was a flash of something that stirred his memory. Something about her fierce face itched at a recollection in the back of his mind. Had he seen this girl before?

"Do I know you?"

"Don't flatter yourself. I'm not one of your groupies." She narrowed her eyes.

"Yeah, good thing. I might find myself as a voodoo doll full of pins if you were in charge of my fan club."

She thought about that for a moment and then laughed. It was such an unexpected sound that it startled him, and for some reason, he started laughing too.

"What?" he said, unable to hold it back any longer.

"You look like the Loch Ness monster."

"You don't look so hot yourself," he shot back, but boy, was he lying. She looked more than hot.

He laughed harder when he noticed his shoes, and how they were no longer a butter-yellow leather. It wasn't that funny, but there was something about laughing after this long, horrible day, added on top of three long, horrible months, that had him chuckling until he bent at the knees. He couldn't stop. His side threatened to ache from it.

Journey just watched him, her brown eyes narrowed at first, finally giving way to a broad smile on her face. When he looked up, he knew she thought he'd seriously lost his marbles, but the truth was, it had been a long time since he'd felt like laughing. Even before the DUI, the judge's verdict, and the months in rehab. So long since he'd even smiled that he couldn't remember when he'd stopped or why. The truth of it sobered him right up, and he straightened, feeling just a little embarrassed.

"You okay?"

Her voice was tentative, searching under the mud and the possibly hysterical laughter.

He shrugged, wiping his eyes and then wiping them again when he got more muck in than out. "Not sure."

He watched her dig a toe of her sneaker into the slime. Ugh. He was such a mess. She peeked over at him.

"I'm not going to ask you if you want to talk about it."

He barked another laugh. This was one girl who didn't do or say anything he thought she would.

"Good."

"Great," she breathed out. Awkward was one way to describe this moment. "Okay, now that we've settled this, I'll show you the lake."

She turned and started to walk, or at least squish, not to the Ranger but up and out of the little meadow valley they were in. She turned back once, her chestnut hair swinging mud in little droplets as she did. "Are you coming? `Cause you're not getting back in the Ranger like that."

He sighed and hauled himself up the hill. In just a few steps he saw what she was talking about. A lake glittered in a long yawn before him, tugging out memories of home and the lake he and his dad used to spend hours on every summer. She turned back once to make sure he was coming and then took off running. The sound of muddy jeans cut through the air until she reached the end of the pier and dove in.

Man, he needed a date. That was the only explanation for the way his insides were kicking up all kinds of dust. He didn't like brunettes. He liked leggy blondes who lived for a good time. He didn't like feisty, mudslinging girls. No. This girl was trouble and then some. And he'd had about enough of trouble for a good long while.

But thinking of how he didn't like her reminded him of the girl he *had* liked and the way she bailed on him the moment he hit rock bottom. The realization sunk like a boulder into the pit of his stomach and made him wish he hadn't stopped drinking.

Journey's head came up out of the water, shooting off sparks of sunshine. "Come on! Don't be chicken!"

A chicken? He was moving in the next moment, the mud that was already starting to dry cracking as he did. He slowed at the pier and then launched himself cannon ball style into the water.

Oh, man! She'd failed to mention he'd be jumping into a bucket of ice overnighted from the North Pole. He came up sputtering and gasping for breath, but she was gone.

"You're gonna have to scrub to get that stuff out of your hair," she called from the deck.

"It's a fricken iceberg in here!"

She laughed. "Welcome to Snowflake Falls, Blake. Mountain water means cold times ten. You'll love it after a long hike during the heat of the day."

He splashed a stream of cold water at her, but she just side stepped it. She'd undone her hair and gathered it over one shoulder as she laid herself down on the pier to warm under the sun. Good idea. He ducked under one more time, bracing himself against the frigid water so he could rub the mud from his face and hair. He made quick work of it, wishing he'd dressed way lighter as his clothes soaked through. Now he'd never get dry, and there was no way he was stripping down to his skivvies with this girl around. He didn't know if he could take her cut downs on his physique.

Within minutes, he was back up on the pier, daring to flop down next to her after he showered her with a shake of his too-long dark hair. She didn't even bother to be annoyed.

"Done being a jerk?" She asked after a moment.

"Probably not." He didn't dare look at her, but he heard the exasperated breath she let out.

"Lucky for you, I'm a nice person, and I won't make you freeze to death on your first day. Come on."

She got up, and he watched. Such a mistake. If his old girlfriend was city lights and pounding music, this girl was clear mountain air and an ice-cold punch in the face. So why was he having such a hard time keeping his eyes off her?

After reminding himself how long he'd been away and attributing his attraction to that, he got up.

"Come on, Cowboy. Let's get you back to your cabin."

He was a coward. He wanted to ask her how he knew her. But the truth was, there were so many girls that he'd briefly met and probably treated badly, even when he was with Tiffany. In the light of a country afternoon, it made him feel ashamed. His mama would be disappointed. She and his stepdad, Trevor, had taught him how to treat a lady. They'd been his biggest cheerleaders in the early years when he was trying to get noticed. Now, he barely spoke to them. The memory of his mother's face at the hearing made him want to crawl into a hole and have a drink.

He shook his head. Not a drink. Good grief. That's what had gotten him into this whole mess. He was beginning to realize how often he turned to a bottle to cope.

The ride back was a blur. He knew he would need to pay better attention tomorrow in order to lead a group to the lake again. But when he got to the cabin he was ready to bolt. Something about being with Journey messed with his focus. He was in the door before he heard his name. "Yeah?" He turned back, trying not to shiver from the chill of his clothes pressing ice cubes to his skin.

"The inn at 7 PM for our planning meeting?"

"Planning?"

She rolled her eyes at him, putting a hand on her hip from where she stood up in the Ranger. "You're here for 'community service,'" she did annoying air quotes, "and that means we're working together every night to plan our next day's excursions. Or did you miss that part of the agreement?"

Man, she was a pain in the …

"Okay, right. I'm just staving off hypothermia."

She smirked. "I'll notify the morgue."

He closed the door and found out how hot the shower could go. It was such a drag that every time he tried to think of his old girlfriend, he saw Journey's sassy smirk instead.

❧✼✼✼☙

"Did you just …?" Ruby gasped, her spatula raised in the air like a weapon. She was in the middle of smashing a heated iron over a sandwich when Journey walked into the kitchen with towel dried hair. Ruby's blue eyes had widened, her pretty little mouth falling open in shock.

"Are you really asking me that? Give me a break. He is the opposite of my type. I'm mostly restraining myself from physical battery when we're in the same room. He's such an ass."

"Cody Blake? No!" Her expression was skeptical. She was used to the billboard, not the human.

"Oh, yes." Journey assured her. "He's an idiot."

Ruby looked confused. "He seemed really nice."

"He seemed like a jerk." Journey hiked her tiny frame up on the barstool and leaned forward. "But that smells wonderful. Whatcha makin'?"

"So that's it, no explanation?" Ruby was offended, and it showed in the way she lifted the iron.

Journey shrugged. "I shoved him into a mud puddle."

Another dramatic gasp. Ruby was such a good listener.

"If you make me one of those ..."

"Paninis?"

"Oh, is that what that is? I just thought it was a sandwich that crossed you and got the hot heavy iron for punishment. But it smells so good."

"Sourdough, deli meats, provolone, a little pesto, thin sliced tomatoes, and onion." Ruby wrote poetry with every word and Journey leaned into it.

"Pretty please?"

"Panzanella, too?"

"What does that even mean?" Journey was sure she'd gone off into Italian again.

Ruby giggled, forgetting to remove the hot iron until the scent of burning brought her back to the task at hand. With a yip she hurried to rescue it, crumbling off the dark edges and placing the sandwich on a plate before turning back to Journey with an explanation.

"I'm sure it roughly translates into "happiness in a salad." Tomatoes, red onion, red wine vinegar, bruschetta, and basil."

"Mmm," Journey groaned, her stomach growling in agreement. "I'm never going to recover from this, Rubes. My jeans actually yelled at me this morning."

"You could start running again."

Journey frowned. Her first try at actual exercise had not been very pleasant. She wasn't used to it. She was used to being perennially hungry and stick skinny. In fact, Wednesdays were always fast days in preparation for the weekend of parties. Coffee, tea, and a lot of caffeine to impersonate the energy that food would give her—that was her life while she was a social-media superstar. Now, she was sitting up at the counter in the kitchen with her elbows planted on either side of her plate.

"I'll think about it."

"You think about it while you tell me every last detail, especially of how amazing Cody looked in wet blue jeans."

She snorted. But with Ruby feeding her deliciousness, she melted into compliance. She told her everything, from bowling into the mud puddle, to the mud splat fight, to calling a truce and the crazy laughing. She didn't linger there, because it still made her feel funny inside. Grandma would have called it her conscience, and if she were here, she would have smacked Journey upside the head. Well, no. Grandma didn't smack. But maybe she should have.

"You get that feeling when God has something for you to do," Grandma would say. "It's a little nudge from the Guy upstairs, and it's usually in a way that you can help one of your fellow men. If you're smart, you won't ignore it."

"Because then Karma will come beat you up with a baseball bat?" Journey had asked.

Grandma's laugh was sunshine and heart. "No, honey. Because sometimes, the very best things happen when you listen to that feeling."

Journey shook off the memory and tamped down the guilt that gathered in her stomach. Okay, the guy had a nice laugh. It was like he'd been hiding it for a long time. And there was something inside of her that wanted to hear it again. But since she'd already decided she disliked him, it was more likely that she'd end up hearing his favorite expletives than laughter in the weeks to come.

She polished off her salad and finished the story.

"And then I drove him back so he wouldn't turn into a snowman."

"Oh, like Olaf. All warm and huggy? How sweet." Ruby looked a little hopeful. Journey wanted to let her down easy.

"Rubes, he's a dirtbag. I can't emphasize this enough. He's the biggest butthead I've ever met."

"I didn't hear one thing about him being less than a gentleman, Journey girl. I think you might just like him."

Journey was disgusted. "I'm not even dignifying that with a response, though I will beg you for a piece of your lemon cream pie?"

She knew she shouldn't add that to the delicious sandwich and tomato salad, but pies were Ruby's specialty. She had a different one up for service every single weekday. Ruby gave her an indulgent smile and began to plate up a slice with a whispered admonition.

"Just be nice, Journey. I mean, the guy's just been in rehab for three months. That's a long stint. Add on some community service away from his family and everyone he's used to having around him. He's got to be lonely."

The pendant lights cast an angelic glow around Journey, but she didn't feel anywhere near angelic, even after breaking loose on Cody. She had a few choice words piling up behind her lips until Ruby swirled just the right amount of whipped cream on top of her slice of lemon pie and slid it in front of her with a little wide-eyed smile. "Now, settle down, sister. I didn't say you needed to make out with him. I'm just saying: be nice."

"I am nice."

Ruby cut her a look before handing off a clean fork.

"Speak of the devil, and listen to what comes on!" Ruby hurried into the kitchen and turned up the radio so it was blasting. Several guests who had wandered in for dinner turned their heads toward the music.

"Ugh! Turn it down. Cody Blake is everything that is wrong with country music!" Journey almost jumped over the counter, but decided the guests would like it better if her once muddy sneakers weren't flying around their food. She opted for darting around it to wrestle Ruby over the buttons.

A deep voice cleared itself nearby.

"You ladies need a hand?"

Ruby went quiet as a mouse while stars boinged from her eyes. Boo. Cody Blake again. Journey turned to see him. He'd trimmed his overgrown beard to something bordering on attractive. His dark hair was still too long and curling over his ears, but at least he'd taken time to make it presentable. His light blue eyes were taking in the scene behind the counter with something like humor crinkling the edges of his eyes. Hmm, he could smile without mud in his face. This was a newsflash.

"Hi, Cody," Ruby breathed.

"Is it seven already?" Journey countered.

Cody grimaced, and Journey was pretty sure that her face made him just as unhappy as his made her.

"Ten minutes to. I'm gonna eat, but we can start going over the outline right now if you don't mind joining me."

She wanted to groan. Ruby was dying. She'd have dinner with Cody Blake in a heartbeat. "I'll grab the tablet."

Dinner with Cody wasn't the worst thing ever. Journey had imagined Neanderthal behavior, lack of napkin skills, and general mouth gaping. But Cody actually knew how to put food into his mouth without being a complete imbecile. Shocker.

"So, that's about it. Four excursions tomorrow and two quad outings we could do on the Diamond trail that goes up by Meadow Bridge."

"We didn't see that today, did we?" Cody was finishing off the last traces of his pie and yes, he almost licked the plate, but Journey couldn't blame him for that.

"Nope. We stopped a bit lower at the lake."

He cleared his throat. "Yeah, I remember that pretty clearly."

Journey let a broad smile fill her face before ducking her head and checking through the last few reservations. "It looks like a full day. I'll see you here at 8 AM."

"Eight?"

He looked tired. His eyes were red rimmed, and Journey was pretty sure he wanted a drink more than anything.

"Sharp." She stood up and strode to the back door as quickly as her short legs could take her. There was that nudge again. The one that had her feeling like she should reach across the table and touch his hand. Agh! What the heck? She did *not* like this jerk. The rush of cold mountain air that hit her skin swept that feeling away and brought her back to herself, but she still needed something more. Moments later, flashlight in her pocket, hoodie over her head, she left the glowing lights of her cabin porch and disappeared into the night.

༄❋❋❋༅

Bright moonlight spilled down on the path, making a flashlight useless. Journey preferred the glow of the moon. It felt like a light from heaven guiding her way, and somehow, it made her feel like Grandma was walking beside her.

It was during moments like these that she could talk to Grandma out loud, not caring if anyone heard her.

"This has been so crazy, Grandma," she started, hands shoved into her pockets, air puffing through her lips because of the high altitude. The rushing of water soon filled the night air and muffled her whispered conversation. She told Grandma everything. About the history she had with Cody. About how much she didn't like him. About the mud, the lake, the feeling. When she finished, she was on the bridge, her hands clasping the railing while dark water glistened in the moonlight below her.

Her voice was too soft to be heard by anyone above the sounds of rushing water. The moonlight washed her hair silver, the chill of the mountain air settling into her skin and raising up goosebumps now that she wasn't walking to keep herself warm.

"I guess what I'm saying is ... I wish you were here. Somehow, you helped me make sense of things like this." She pushed a hand through her hair that had dried in messy waves and sighed. Looking up at the moon surrounded by a sky exploding with stars, she settled in to think. She knew she only had about thirty minutes before she would be too cold to make her brain function, even in her hoodie, but she hoped it would be enough.

She walked to the other side of the bridge and slid down to her bottom, wrapping her arms around herself and letting her head rest against the cold metal of the railing. This was how it worked. Talking from her and then quiet thinking. Though Grandma wasn't here anymore to help her sort through the emotions that clouded her judgment, up here she always felt near.

"You know ... it wouldn't hurt to give a little."

The thought came as clearly as the others. A little whisper just above the sound of the water.

She snorted. Yeah, right. Give a little? Why? He's not worth it. If you'd met him this afternoon, you would understand. But Grandma's voice came back more clearly this time.

"Pardon me, cupcake, but every living soul is worth it. And don't you forget it."

Ugh.

She wasn't ready to give up this fight.

That's always when it happened. A memory or experience would come to her mind, like a bit of gold settling down to the bottom of a pan when the silt and sand had drifted away.

This memory opened on a morning soon after her arrival in Gunlock to stay with her grandma. She hadn't exactly had a choice in the matter, and the tension between her and a woman she didn't know well could be felt in the air.

Isabelle was used to almost constant conflict and underhanded criticism in her life with Helen. The fact that Grandma was so different felt like a trick. Journey could remember thinking that maybe her grandma was complaining about her behind her back instead of saying it outright. She was just waiting for the other shoe to drop. The strain between them was incredible. Each time Grandma would do something nice for her, she would snap back, hoping to draw her out of her polite mode and start getting real.

Seeing herself from the perspective of time, Journey couldn't believe her grandma was so patient with such a snarky, whiny teenager.

It was mid-summer; the days were too warm to stay indoors, yet Isabelle was still recovering from a recent appendectomy and couldn't do much.

"You know, you'd enjoy yourself more if you actually picked up one of those books." Grandma pointed her chin toward the small tower stacked at random on her night table.

Isabelle didn't look away from her phone, even as Grandma slid a tray onto her lap. Everything smelled good, but nothing *tasted* good. It was frustrating. Grandma said it was the meds. Mealtimes became an exercise in disappointment.

"No, thanks. I'm ... not hungry."

"Want to talk about it?"

Isabelle shook her head, still glued to the screen in her hand. It was her go-to method for dealing with uncomfortable situations. This time, Grandma snatched her phone and held it out of reach. Stretching was impossible after having her body hacked open and sewn back together, so Isabelle settled for her best pout.

"You can't take my phone, you know."

"I don't have any intention of keeping it if we can create some agreeable boundaries."

Her face was calm. Isabelle was sure a tirade was coming any minute, but no. Just that relaxed, determined voice.

"Are you ... going to start screaming?"

Grandma chuckled, pushing up her dark rimmed glasses. "I gave that up when I was about fifteen."

Isabelle fidgeted. It felt weird not to have a device in her hands to distract her. "I know you don't want me here."

"Who told you that?" Grandma looked genuinely surprised, her brows drawn up, her brown eyes widened.

"No one has to *tell* me. It's pretty obvious. I don't see you for six years, and all of a sudden, we're doing summer camp together. We both wish I was back in the city where I belong." There, it was out.

Grandma's brows slowly lowered, and she studied the phone in her hands before locking eyes with Isabelle. "You belong where your heart is," Grandma said, "and where you feel loved the best. I'm doing all I can to help you feel loved, but it's hard when we know so little about each other."

Isabelle's face was skeptical. "Knowing me better won't make you love me more."

"Says who?"

Isabelle threw up her hands in frustration. Then the words she hadn't meant to say came spilling out. "My own mom dropped me off for the summer because I'm too much of a ... what did she call it? Distraction? Trouble? Problem? *She* knows me better than anyone. If she doesn't want me, why would you?"

Isabelle thought her grandma caught her breath, but she didn't break. When she spoke, there was a hint of steel in her words. "My daughter has found herself in the distinctly poor position of being distracted from what matters most. Happens to the best of us, honestly, but I'll not make excuses for her. What I'll do is make you a deal. You let me in, just on a trial basis. Let me get to know you like I've wanted to since the day you were born, and then we'll see where home is. Fair enough? If you still want to go back to the city once you get doctor's clearance, I'll make sure it happens."

Isabelle considered it, weighing all the pros and cons in her head as best she could. Her skull always started to pound when she got too worked up over something before eating.

"Okay, fine."

Grandma's smile was radiant. "I'll start with this get-to-know-you business by sharing a song I like. Maybe you could share one of yours when I'm through?"

Isabelle settled in, trying to make herself eat something from the tray in front of her. Again, the taste was flavorless. She was pretty sure Grandma could cook, because the smells coming from her kitchen were nothing short of heaven. She only wished she could *taste* it.

The song that Grandma played, then, came back to her with crystal clarity, even now on the mountain beneath a blanket of starry skies. It was by Joe Diffy, a '90s country artist with a long list of hits. She didn't know that then. What she knew was that her grandma turned on something she hadn't really heard much of before. It was a ballad, and the words told a story that unfolded in her mind with every verse. Each chorus begged the listener not to laugh or make fun of those who struggle in life. In God's eyes we all have worth and one day we'll be free of these limitations.

A wave of goosebumps washed over her from head to toe, and Journey blinked back the surge of emotion that memory brought to the surface.

"I hear you," she whispered, all her bravado and angst evaporated into the cold night's air. Okay, so maybe she didn't have to love everything about the pain-in-the-butt country superstar in the cabin beside hers, but maybe she could find a way to be kind. To remember that everyone has value. Her breath came out in a crystal puff as she stood, doing some high knees to restore circulation and warm up her frigid limbs.

"Grandma, I miss you," she whispered, her voice lifting up on the warmth of her breath and rising toward the stars.

ಬಿ✵✵✵ೆ

Outside his window, the world had dunked itself in blackest ink with only the thin lines of twinkle lights on the porch of each cabin to break up the darkness. The only other lights came from the windows of the inn, golden pools in the distance, and the one cabin behind his where music was playing loud enough for him to catch a melody line here and there. It wasn't loud enough to distract him, though, and it wasn't the reason he was up tonight, pacing.

He'd done well in rehab, really. Even though he was a pain in the butt to everyone who came into his room, and gave his therapists hell. When it came down to it, no one wants to be an alcoholic. He wanted to kick this. Well, he did after the first three weeks, anyway. Directly following a brutal week in prison to help refresh his determination. Yeah. After that experience scared the crap out of him, he was a lot more willing. And he'd done the program—even buying into the need for a higher power in his life—doing all the steps and writing in his notebook about his progress. All of it.

But tonight, the craving for a drink to knock him numb hit him like a truck.

Maybe it was the fact that Tiffany wouldn't return his calls. Maybe it was the fact that he'd gotten desperate enough to call her even when he knew. Maybe it was the lyrics running around in his head like they had when he was a kid until he thought he'd lose his mind. The words that hit his heart but did nothing to sell his brand. He'd learned a long time ago to ignore them. Music execs didn't want heartfelt country anymore. They wanted shocking, genre bending songs with larger-than-life personalities.

Yet his fingers itched to write them down. The words that kept looping through his brain with no alcohol to quiet them. Even though he knew he had nothing, he'd gone through all his luggage already, throwing it around the room like a maniac, just hungry for a little something. He'd even toyed with the ludicrous idea of rooting around the kitchen.

He dialed his sponsor but couldn't get a decent signal. His phone left a dent in the wall. He sank down with his head in his hands just as someone pounded on his door.

Cody looked around in a panic. He was in his sweat pants and an old tee from his high school days. Go Groundhogs! But man, the place was a mess. This was it. Ben was going to kick him out the minute he saw it and send him back to jail to finish out his extended sentence like the judge had warned him. He thought for a minute about pretending to be asleep, but the phone into the wall moments before probably gave away how awake he was.

His brain spun some kind of excuse about the state of his room and the cracked screen on his smart phone lying on the ground. But when he opened the door, he only saw her.

Chapter Five

Journey Miller stood in the muted glow of his porch lights. She had one ear bud in her ear, the other dangling hot pink onto her pajama tank top. Cupped in her hand was a music player, and on her face, the scowl he was coming to know quite well. The shock of seeing her there in her pajamas with her hair in some kind of messy twist on top of her head knocked the thought of drinking right out of his brain.

"This. Are you serious? *This* is what killed country. Dead. Worse than assassination. More like a totally gruesome homicide with *your* fingerprints everywhere." Her accusing finger was inches from his chest, her dark eyes flaying him in one glance.

"What … are you talking about?" He was baffled by her fury. And his screaming brain was having trouble switching gears from tortured to defensive. Something about country music? What?

"Don't act like you don't know." She pushed passed him and into his cabin, stopping short as her eyes grew wide with the mess. Her assessment didn't take long to come back. "You're a pig, Blake. Jeez. You've been here like twelve hours, and this is what you're going for? Catastrophic chic?"

"My suitcase blew up?"

She blinked at him. "A smart aleck. Great. Listen to this."

It was a demand. She shoved the ear bud that had been dangling down on her shirt toward him, and he took it with a step forward. That step brought him close enough to be reminded of their earlier wrestle in the mud when he had her pinned to his chest.

Good grief, she smelled amazing. One of his favorite scents, orangey citrus, exploded over his senses. He held his breath and plugged the headphone in one ear. Bouncing back at him was one of his latest releases. It was on top of the charts when he went into rehab. It gave him a boost of excitement to hear it again and a sliver of hope that it was still faring well. He grinned, starting to bob his head along with the beat. He had to admit it wasn't the typical country he'd grown up with, not even close to the music he wrote for years after school with his guitar. It had a rap section that the rapper, DownBeat, had guested on. It was definitely genre bending.

She popped the earbud out of his ear with a little yank. "You call that country?"

She had to tip her head back to look up into his face this close. He noticed that her dark brown eyes were circled by a charcoal black ring. Attention, Cody. He started breathing again.

"It's on the top of the charts as far as I know."

"It has *rap* in it." The word fell from her lips in a disgusted drop.

"Yeah, with DownBeat, one of the hottest rappers out there. Do you know what my agent had to do to make that happen?"

She took a step closer, her eyes narrowing. "You seem to forget that we're supposed to be singing *country*. Songs that mean something. Lyrics that tell a story and wake you up. If you want to be a pop star or break into the rap market with cookie cutter repeat lyrics, go for it. But *don't* label it country."

"Did I mention it's *top selling*?" He was having a hard time concentrating on the argument, not only because Journey was all up in his business, but she was so passionate about it he could almost feel the waves of disdain rippling off her tiny frame. And it totally got his attention in a way that took him completely off guard. He still didn't like her, but there was something innately captivating about her. The fact that she literally hated him felt amazingly authentic and refreshing after the hordes of girls who threw themselves at him.

"The only reason this trash is on top is because no one remembers the good songs anymore." She threw up a hand and turned her back on him.

He shook his head. "And why did you say *we're* supposed to be singing country?"

She shot him a look over her shoulder, "I said you."

"No, you said *we*."

"You're full of crap, just like this freaking travesty of a song that you put out." She turned on him, and he just let her come. "It's people like you that screw up nice things. You, singing every song about these imaginary, half-naked, sex-crazed, blondes and then throwing rap or pop into it. Whatever happened to the basics of country that happen to include *respecting* women and having some religion? You're obliterating it. Do you know that the average city kid wouldn't even know the difference between your song and the other trash being played on the radio these days?"

"Isn't that a good thing? Wouldn't I want to sell to everyone on the planet, not just a select group of country-loving people? I mean, twenty years ago, country was a minority. People joked about playing it backwards and getting your dog back, your wife back, and sober."

"So this is a money thing." Her brown eyes narrowed, and he knew he was on dangerous ground. The mud puddle had taught him this and yet …

"Sweetheart, it's always about money."

The look in her eyes was half disappointment and half fury. He didn't know which scared him more as she advanced on him, pressing her finger into his chest, directly in the middle over his breastbone.

"First of all," she was whispering, and he would be lying if it didn't make his heart race, "if you call me sweetheart, ever again, I'll make you regret it. And second, *nothing* worth doing is about the money. Nothing. It never has been and it never will be. Sometimes good money is the byproduct of living a life you can be proud of. Sometimes it isn't, but the end result is the same. At the end of the day you have something you can be proud to have your name on."

The fury left her eyes by the last sentence, and she was incredibly sincere.

He couldn't believe how mesmerized he was by her intensity. Every quick comeback fled in the face of her earnestness. Her eyes were so deep he thought he could fall into them and never find his way out. It was in that moment that her eyes flicked to his mouth. His heart skipped a beat. But she was already moving away, her expression a mixture of confusion and amusement.

"You need to clean this place up, Blake. And maybe just think about singing something that doesn't murder an entire genre in cold blood."

She blazed out of his cabin, and he just stood there, the smell of citrus bruising the air around him. One good thing: he wasn't thinking about a drink anymore.

୬୦✳✳✳୧୯

Journey gunned the quad she was on, catching up with Cody who sat on the side of the trail letting the rest of the group go ahead.

"Taking a brain break?"

She couldn't see his expression behind his pilot sunglasses. "Waiting on you, princess."

"Oh, don't try the Han impression, Blake. You can't pull it off."

He smirked at her. "Do you ever take your foot off the sarcasm pedal, Journey?"

She returned his smirk and raised him an eyebrow. "You bring it out in me."

He shook his head and she almost felt bad for being such a pain. The thing was, something had happened last night. In the middle of calling him on his crap, there had been this moment when she'd felt a flash of brilliant attraction. Something about the look on his face, and the warmth of his chest under her finger, had taken her by surprise, and for one second, her mind had wandered to what it might feel like to kiss him.

She was absolutely disgusted with herself. To be honest, he was a total player. She had seen the reports about the number of girls he went through, all tall, blond, party girls. Even if she was stupid enough to think he was anything more than a bad-boy attraction, the bold, bright facts remained that the minute he left Snowflake Falls, he was headed head-first back into the business that he loved.

"I just wanted to say something about last night."

Journey shot him a look. She'd nurtured the crazy hope that he hadn't noticed. Yeah, of course he did. Stupid slip up!

"Why don't we do our job and forget about last night." Journey gave it some gas, but Cody caught up to her easily.

"There's nothing wrong with singing what sells. Everyone does it."

"You do what you want." Journey shrugged. "I just thought you might be interested in staying true to what launched you in the first place. As much as I hate to admit it, your first album wasn't horrible."

Cody looked surprised and fell behind for a moment before hitting the throttle to catch back up.

"You mean that?"

She cut him a sharp look. She wasn't trying to kiss his butt. She was being honest. "I don't want to marry you over it, cowboy."

He tipped his baseball cap back. "You have a hard time being nice, don't you?"

"You'd be amazed at how pleasant I can be with people who don't make me want to hurl all the time."

Zing! But this time, it didn't feel as good when it hit home. No, it only tasted like guilt. She could almost see her grandma's disapproving glance. But dang it! It was harder to be nice in real life than in her good intentions on the bridge.

He gunned his quad this time, and they finished the tour without speaking, parking their off roaders in the big barn out back. Journey blew out a breath and bit the bullet. Her grandma's words about being kind had been ringing in her ears the entire ride home. Before he could stomp off, she grabbed his arm. "Blake, wait. I'm sorry. I don't like you. But my grandma would be so disappointed if she ever heard me talk to someone like that."

He looked down at her and then away. "Is that an apology or an insult? I'm just not sure how to read it, Journey."

She shrugged. "It's a truce. We don't have to be besties, but I'm willing to try to be cordial."

He grinned. "Cordial."

"I won't try to insult you with every other word," she amended, "but I don't like you."

"Why's that?" He'd stepped closer. It shouldn't have been disconcerting, but it was. He was still the same cocky jerk who'd come into town the day before.

"I ... just don't," she said, stepping back to preserve the distance between them. "I'll be nice if you can try not to be an idiot."

"And, there it is." He was grinning now. "You can't help yourself."

"I'll do what I can." She turned then, desperate to get away from him.

"Going in to have dinner?"

She was famished, but she didn't want to make a habit of eating with him. It felt too close to comfortable for her taste.

"I'm gonna clean up first."

He shrugged. "Suit yourself. I thought you'd be starving."

She could kick herself. Ugh. Now she had to shower on an empty stomach. She walked into her cabin regretfully, turned on some music as loud as she could, and hit the shower. On the way to the bathroom, she found an extra slice of lemon bread that Ruby had sent her home with last night. Thank goodness. As lemon crumbs melted on her tongue and calmed her grumbling tummy, Journey decided she would find a way to pay Ruby back. It was the least she could do to thank her friend for saving her from starvation while she avoided Cody Blake.

❧❃❃❃☙

Two weeks later, Lucille met Journey at the barn. Journey pulled off her helmet and shook out her hair, wiping her forehead on her sleeve.

"Done with the Moens?" Lucille was holding two large, sweating mason jars of lemonade, turned pink by the strawberry chunks swimming inside. Journey grinned, stepping off the quad and setting her helmet down.

"Yes. They loved that trail."

"These have been a good investment." Lucille nodded toward the parked off-roaders. "They take some care, but they're fun for our guests."

Offering one glass to Journey, she nodded toward the back porch of the inn, and Journey followed her, drinking in the delicious refreshment. For the last few months, this had become a bit of a thing between them. Every week or so, Lucille would come find her, and they'd have a very casual interview of sorts.

At first, Journey had felt guarded and uncertain about where the conversation was going. But now, these talks made her feel so much like home, it was hard not to think of her grandma sitting there beside her.

Settling into matching Adirondacks on the back porch, Lucille took a sip of lemonade before turning to her with a questioning look on her face.

"I'm curious how the last two weeks have compared to your first months here at the inn."

Journey couldn't help the smile that came to her face. "Quads and sunshine beat toilets any day."

Lucille laughed, nodding her head in agreement. "Never has a truer statement been made. I guess I was prying more into the setup between you and Mr. Blake. I heard … there was mud."

Journey chewed her lip for a minute, trying to determine whether she was in trouble or not. "He was being a jerk, Mama. And it only happened once."

"Now, I am surprised." Lucille's smile was warm. "You have way more self-control than I gave you credit for."

Journey stopped trying to explain and tipped her head. "You're not mad?"

Lucille laughed again. "I considered something of that kind myself that first day."

Now, it was Journey's turn to laugh. They both took a sip of lemonade before Journey went on. "I guess he's fine. Full of himself. A complete mess in a lot of things. But, if I'm being fair, he's great with the guests, even without them knowing he's "The Cody Blake". I mean, he charms the socks off every lady who walks in, and the guys think he's cool too."

"And you?"

Journey thought she was pretty plain with an eye roll. She took a long tart-sweet sip of juice and then sighed, meeting Lucille's cornflower blue eyes. "Like I said, he's so much better than toilets."

Lucille laughed, tipping her head back for a moment, the evening sunshine catching the glints of copper in her hair. "Well, that's something."

She nodded, collecting her thoughts for a moment and then leaned forward like she did when she wanted to share something important. Journey braced herself.

"There's been something brewin' in the back of my mind for days now, and I guess I oughta get to sharin' it so my brain can rest on the matter."

Journey nodded, clasping the glass on her thigh, letting the beaded droplets of water pool in a circle on her jeans.

"You know what I've learned from being alive as long as I have? There are not many people on the planet you can hate once you know their story. I see from the look on your face that you dispute that sentiment, but maybe this experience I had when I was a young mother of three busy kids will help you understand what I'm sayin'.

At that time, I was introduced to a woman. She was tall and slender, and her style was sharp. Man, I didn't think we could possibly have anything in common. But we went to the same church, and as fate would have it, we ended up on the same committee. I was certain I could not like her. Though I considered myself a Christian woman, I was throwing out judgments left and right without even knowin' it.

"I think my young heart felt threatened by the woman she was. While I was at home with the kids, she was out in the business world. She was an artist, and that was part of everything she did. It showed in her style, in her hair, in the eclectic clothes she wore, and even in the way she walked. It was like a dance, where mine was more a hurdle to the finish line with kids pulling on all my appendages." Lucille chuckled at the comparison.

"Looking back, I can see that her bright, unapologetic life made me ashamed of hiding in mine. I'd made excuses about what I wanted to do with my life. I'd necessarily put aside some of my hobbies for my little ones.

"Now, don't think I'm apologizin' for that. Those are the kinds of sacrifices you treasure. Yet, at that time in my life, I wasn't being authentic to who I needed to be. Well, being on that committee, rubbing shoulders with this woman who was real to the very core of her soul ... Journey, it changed me. I could no longer judge her from afar when I was lovin' her more every moment we spent together. With those moments, I was learning her story.

"And what a story it was. She was a young mother with four growing children, when her husband, after much sacrifice and effort on everyone's part, graduated from years of dental school. Finally, they could work toward their goals and enjoy the fruits of his labors. Only three months later, he was killed unexpectedly in a plane crash. Overnight, this woman was a widow and provider. Despite her mourning, she drew herself up, threw herself into her passion, got further training, and did all she could to support her family. And in the midst of it, she found love again despite insurmountable odds."

"Wow." Journey was consumed in the story, imagining every detail that Lucille's words painted for her.

"Yeah, wow indeed. That woman transformed how I viewed my life, my goals, my dreams. Suddenly, I had no excuses to ignore my passions. And in the same breath, my husband became more dear and my family treasured. I thanked God for His wisdom in bringing this unexpected friend into my life."

Lucille stirred her lemonade for a moment, mingling the strawberry and lemon juices as she did so.

"I guess what I'm sayin' is that, sometimes, we need to know someone's story before we make those judgment calls. Is the reason we don't like someone because of the passionate way they live their lives? Humans tend to like hiding for some reason. Hidin' from their purpose, their bliss. We get afraid and we draw our heads in like a turtle. But her story also showed me the delicacy of life. That was the year I stopped bein' afraid to enjoy dessert."

Journey laughed. "I'm way ahead of you on that one." She patted her thigh to show the results of her efforts.

Lucille laughed too. "Oh, Ruby will do that to you, won't she? Don't get me wrong, I still like to fit into my jeans, but I've learned to cherish the opportunities that life throws my way. They come when I'm not plannin' on 'em, so I have to be flexible and trust my gut. Journey, I hope you can do the same."

Something about the way Lucille spoke shook down all the barriers that would have popped up from anyone else. As she stood to go, tapping her soft, slender fingers over Journey's, Journey felt something like a swell in her chest; like her heart was enlarging to accept everything that Lucille had shared. A flash of goose bumps raced over her.

Grandma like to call that feeling lightning bugs. That flash, and then the rush of energy over her skin. *"When you feel the lightning bugs, it means something important is happening. Pay attention. That is heaven talkin' to ya, and you don't dismiss heaven."*

Journey let the feeling sink in, let Lucille's words soak into her skin and settle into her bones just like the warmth of sunshine that lingered after a long day. Those words made the walk back to her cabin much longer. Did something about Cody make her feel threatened? Did it remind her of her own dismissed passions? The way she threw aside what felt right to be part of her family?

Lightning bugs again!

She rubbed her bumpy arms and hurried into her cabin. There in the corner was her thrift-store guitar. It needed tuning. But for some reason, tonight she didn't put it off like she had ever since getting it on the way to Snowflake Falls. Instead, she sat down on her couch and pulled it onto her lap.

It had been about three years since she'd played much of anything. Even more since she had sung something she wanted to sing. Her time in the studio was always with the band backing her up. Helen didn't like her to play an instrument. She said that having it strapped over her shoulder made Isabelle look like a hillbilly.

"We're selling upper class," Helen reminded her. "Not Grandma June's pumpkin stand."

If anyone made her feel fake, it was her mother. In the pursuit of appearing to be the best of everything, Helen had a hard time with what showed up on her doorstep after Grandma passed away. Instead of an Internet sensation, Journey was ... ordinary. She had split ends and torn jeans. And not the fancy torn-for-you jeans. Her mother had pulled her into the house like she was on the witness protection program. Within two hours, she had a new hair color, and Helen was debating what color contacts to order for her.

"We can't have you trailing around us like a country bumpkin. My goodness, your cuticles are enough to have us banned from Jerome's for good."

"Give it a rest, Helen. She's been home five minutes." Jen was much warmer in her greeting than the rest.

"See if Gracio will come right away and do a major mani pedi." Liz was just as alarmed as her mother over Isabelle's average appearance. "And we need Arturo to come do her brows before tomorrow. Oh, my word, it's like she doesn't even look in the mirror."

Journey's laugh was more ironic than amused whenever she studied herself in the mirror now. "Authentic just wasn't part of the business plan, was it?" But Lucille was right. Being the real her was frightening. It was the reason she was here, and yet, she found herself hiding from it just like Lucille had said, afraid to dive in and find out if the real Journey was still inside.

She strummed the strings, loving the feel of the guitar and the memories that seemed to holograph all around her when she touched them. This was what she treasured about music. There was power in it on so many levels. But her guitar was out of tune, and her attempts to get it right only left her frustrated.

She was pretty sure one person could help her get on key. Without debating the idea, Journey put the strap over her shoulder, grabbed the neck where it attached to the base of the guitar, and crossed the gravel to knock on the door of Cabin 5.

Another knock—her foot tapping with impatience—brought a shuffle of feet and Cody Blake … with no shirt on.

Chapter Six

"Hey?" He looked wary, and she couldn't blame him. Okay, so it was obvious he worked out while in rehab. Stop staring, Journey.

"Have a tuning harp on you?"

"A ..." His brows did a good job of finishing off the question. She held up the guitar to answer it.

"I've got A and C, but the others ... they're just off, and the Internet isn't helping."

"You ... play?" He took the guitar from her, his fingers brushing hers as he lifted it over her head.

She ignored the moment and shrugged. "A little."

He motioned her in with his head while twisting some knobs and strumming the metal strings as he worked. She sank down onto his couch, listening to him pick his way through the notes, trying not to overthink the fact that her guitar was touching the bare skin of his very attractive chest. She tried to conjur up her inner snark, but got distracted when she heard him hitting the right tones. He started strumming something familiar.

"Name that tune," he said, his fingers moving over the strings.

Journey shrugged again, reminded of Lucille's words. She was bugged that Cody wasted his talent singing stuff that hurt the genre she loved. But if she was being honest—in her life before this—she had done much of the same thing, ignoring her inner passion to follow the family business of making headlines, whether it included music or not. She was out to sing the latest and most controversial pop music without a care for what it did to the world around her.

Finally, the tune clicked. "You can't be playing Elvis."

"Classic." He grinned. He really did have a nice smile. But even if she was going to heed Lucille's words on knowing a person's story, she wasn't going to like him that much.

"He had a gift," Journey agreed, extending her hand for the guitar. He held it for a minute as if deciding, and then handed it back. It was warm where it had been in his arms. She cradled it, relishing the feel of the strings. With a few false starts, she strummed another tune, and shot him a look to see if he was catching on.

Instead of just calling out the name of the song, he started singing. It was one of her favorite contemporary country groups. Some people still knew how to make good country. However, the combination of him shirtless and singing was really uncomfortable for her. When he reached the end of the first phrase, she stopped playing and jumped up.

"Yep, right on."

"You're going?"

Journey was at the edge of his porch when she turned back. He was leaning against the doorframe, his eyes on her in the barely-there light of the moon hanging out overhead, filtering through the mammoth pine trees and casting shadows. She should have left right then, but a question had been plaguing her, and she blurted it out.

"Why did you do it? What made you change from that first album?"

He crossed his arms over that chest. It was a good look for him. Formidable. Sexy. "Why does it matter, Journey?"

"It's your story, jerk. Why can't you just own up to it instead of making me skewer it out of you?"

A hint of a smile. "No one wanted to hear honest country. You only know about my first album because of the three others after it that hit the charts."

"What about 'He Didn't Have to Be,' by Brad Paisley? Think about it: a first time father remembering the guy who stepped in and became his dad. You don't get more heartfelt than that."

"I wasn't Brad, okay? I was an eager country boy with no backing and no one who cared that I could write or play guitar. One of thousands trying to make it big. What they wanted was a front man, and that's what I gave them."

"You sold out." Journey said it softly, and he shrugged.

"Don't tell me you've never sold out before."

She looked away. She couldn't. She couldn't tell him that because she'd sold out for years. That was the whole reason behind her disappearing. She was trying to remember what it felt like to be authentic even just for herself.

"Well, I just think music can change people. Think about '90s country. I mean, that's when country music gave something back to the world. George Strait, Clint Black, Martina McBride, Reba ... every one of them sang songs that made you feel something," Journey said.

She pulled her guitar to her chest and strummed a few bars and then started to sing. Her voice was full and soft. She sang the first lines of a Judd's song about an age-old photograph that showed a family resemblance through generations. It tugged her mind back to a tiny country home and a woman who loved her the way a grandma should. She paused. "Those songs told a story. I sang that at my grandma's funeral. She was a crazy '90s country fan."

"Nineties had their share of suggestive lyrics too, Journey. Reba sang about prostitutes and murderous sisters."

Journey's eyes narrowed. She strummed her guitar again countering his comment with a new tune. This one was upbeat and sassy. It told of a girl that didn't have to dress like a beauty queen to get the attention of the boy she loved. When she finished singing Journey gave him a look that said, "Whatcha got?"

He shook his head. "Hang on a minute. If we're going to do this, I'm going to need something."

He walked into his room and she watched him go, hoping what he needed was a shirt. The cold mountain air was coming in through the door, so she stepped back in and kicked it shut, just warming up to the idea of battling it out, country music style.

A moment later, she heard the sound of steel strings under fingertips. Cody came out with his own guitar, this one all pop-starred up with cool graphics. She grinned when she heard that it sounded just as good as the one her grandma had bought her the Christmas after she moved in. As a bonus, he had pulled on a black tee shirt. He decided to answer her Martina McBride with some Tim McGraw.

His choice was a song that Journey loved. It painted a humorous picture of an Indian outlaw who was in love with a one of a kind Chippewa lady. He sang it with just enough of a croon to stir something in Journey's chest. She could tell why the girls swooned when he sang that way.

She didn't show how his singing affected her. Instead she executed an eye roll before answering back with a few bars of her own Tim McGraw tune. Her selection reminisced about living where the green grass grows and raising kids where the good Lord's blessed.

The moment she stopped, Cody thundered out an intro and cut into the chorus of a Garth Brooks hit about a trucker who caught his wife cheating. The end of the story had one in the graveyard and one in prison.

Journey matched him right back with the first song that came to mind. This one was just as catchy as Cody's, but it wasn't about a jealous husband. It was about a guy who had found the light and been baptized by the love he felt for his girl. His love was a religious experience.

"Ah, love songs, huh?" He raised his brows and then looked thoughtful while his fingers worked their magic over the strings. "How about this one?" He pulled out a classic, singing from his heart about the kid who climbed a water tower to spray paint I LOVE YOU in John Deere Green. It was his special way of declaring his devotion.

She hit back with a George Strait, like the ace it was. She watched Cody's eyes widen when she sang to him about the note passed between two friends asking the age old questions. "Do you love me?" "Do you wanna be my friend?" You just had to check yes or no on that sweet little note. Journey had to look away when she got to that part. There was something intense in Cody's eyes that she didn't know if she wanted to see.

He cleared his throat and picked at his strings while deliberating over his next choice. He snapped his fingertips. "I got it!" The moves that came with this song had Journey laughing out loud. He sang about Bubba, the guy who secretly bought a video to learn how to dance. Without telling a soul, he learned the two step, the slide, and all the latest dance moves. When he showed them off to his friends, they were shocked by how smooth he could be.

Okay, he was sexy. Bubba had nothing on Cody. Man, even with the too long hair and the beard that he had kept trimmed along his jaw line. Those blue eyes were pretty amazing, if she let herself look at them long enough. And she made sure she didn't.

Instead, she tipped her head back, searching the ceiling for her next song. A Neal McCoy classic popped into her head. She sang of troubles taking a hike without a need for a visit to the shrink, or a drink to make him feel good. All he needed was that special wink from his girl.

Cody chuckled while bringing Garth back into it with his friends in low places.

"Garth again." Journey had to admit this was always a good choice. But so was Faith Hill with her delight over blissful kisses that set her spinning. Singing about watching someone during a sexy kiss may not have been the best choice to keep the mood light. Once again, Cody came to the rescue.

He started tapping his foot, beating a rhythm on his guitar in between chords. He hit her with Billy Ray Cyrus' misunderstanding over his broken achy heart. Even for a 90's country lover like Journey, it was a bit more than she could handle.

Journey held up her hand to stop him. "Okay, fine. Please, I get it. There are some '90s songs that should be left in the nineties, but come on. Don't tell me you don't feel something when Alison Krauss tells you that you say it best without saying a word. Surely that's more romantic than being told to shake your thang to the left and right to attract the boys."

Journey held her arms open with a challenging look.

"You mean, building a bridge from love is more inspiring than making a guy's speakers go boom boom?" His face was impish. He knew full well that the Judds would always beat out everyone else.

"How about being amazed by every little thing your baby does? Who doesn't want to be loved like that?" Journey crooned a few lines of the Lone Star favorite.

He was grinning at her when she finished.

"What?" She suddenly realized they'd been singing love songs to each other for the last ten minutes.

"Nothing. I just ... you have a great voice."

"That's not the point, Blake. The point is, what ever happened to songs like that? Songs about living like you were dying or choosing to dance through the good times and the bad?"

He was shaking his head. "There are still good songs out there, Journey."

She rubbed her hands vertically down the strings on her guitar where it hung from her neck. "Yeah, and there's a lot of garbage too. Turn on the radio and all you'll hear are men sexualizing women into the next one-night stand. Geez, Blake, there's more to life than the party crowd. And when you're the one fronting the band, singing the songs ... I don't know." She paused, and then finished.

"My grandma used to say if you're going to do something big and loud, make sure you'd want your kids to know about it."

That stopped him cold. He looked up from his guitar with something like surprise on his face. She couldn't tell what he was thinking, only that her words had taken him aback.

"Your kids? Seriously?"

She lifted her chin, not backing down an inch. "Seriously. I mean, I want to be a mom someday. I think about some of the dumb things I've done already, and I get what she was saying. I guess it's about being true to yourself. Honoring who we really are. I just don't buy the bad-boy front-man act with you, Cody. I think there's more to you than that. I think that's why you're here. To figure out the real you and be brave enough to live it out loud."

Cody looked at her for a long moment, his brows scrunched together in thought.

She could tell this was one she should let him sleep on, so she strummed her guitar one more time and backed toward the door. "I'm gonna go. But just think about this one from arguably the biggest country star of the 90s, Garth Brooks." She backed out of the room singing about God and how sometimes we have to remember that He's the one in control. When we think He's not hearing our pleas, sometimes He's sending down some of His very best blessings in those prayers that go unanswered.

ಸೋ❋❋❋ಜಿ

"Wow, thanks." Cody held onto the sarcasm as he followed her to the door. He had to work hard to hide how her words hit him, point blank, right through all his defenses. He watched her blend into the shadows of the night, the darkness swallowing her and her guitar until the lights from her porch outlined her figure, and then a brilliant light from her doorway scooped her up and shut her away. He turned back to an empty room where the glow dimmed without her bold personality there. He had definitely not expected to spend a half hour singing songs he knew by heart.

Songs he knew by heart.

Stories that could make him laugh or cry.

Words that meant something.

He picked at the strings on his guitar, his mind blowing up with snippets of songs and their conversation. The way she confronted him with his stupidity and then challenged him to be a better man without even setting off his alarms was ridiculous. He was so off his game.

But her voice. The way she sang … like it saved her life, he thought, wiping his face with both hands. And the way she shot back song after song. He didn't think he had ever had that much fun with a girl. Out of all the people who surrounded him in his life, there was no one that pushed him like she did. And he hated it.

He *wanted* to hate it. He wanted to be bugged by the way she made his life harder than it needed to be. Think about his kids? Come on! He wasn't even dating someone he would think about having kids with. That was years and years away. But there it was, nibbling amoeba-like on his brain.

What if his kids knew *this* Cody Blake? The one who got drunk. All. The. Time. The one who sang songs about getting laid and chasing girls. The one who didn't even know the first place to start being authentic. That—that would suck big time.

He sank down onto the couch, head in his hands. That's when the music started in his head, a haunting tune with words that went through his mind. He closed his eyes tightly, the urge for a drink filling him in one horrible surge. Gritting his teeth, he thought through the steps of his program. He was halfway through them when he pushed his guitar aside, paced to the counter where a pad of stationery embossed with the inn logo sat, and grabbed it, walking to the table. He had to get up a second later for a pen.

This time, when he sat down, he took a deep breath, his hands shaking. It never used to be this difficult. But when inspiration is stamped out enough, it starts to stamp back. He closed his eyes hard again. The words hadn't disappeared. They were louder than ever.

"I'm not the man I want to be,

I've made a few mistakes.

Gone astray, but now I see,

The difference I can make."

When he was done, he slept better than he'd slept in years.

There was pounding somewhere in the distance. If Ian was trying to wake him up early again, he was going to punch him in the nose. Cody turned over. Somewhere in the night, he had lost his shirt. The sound of pounding reached him again. Someone was impatient.

Only, he wasn't in his downtown apartment. He was in Cabin #5. He shook his head, the night before rushing back in quick musical flashes.

"I'm not leaving, Blake."

Journey's voice. With an edge.

He got up, yawning, and then started when he saw his clock. It was 9:49. Holy crap. He was late for work.

He hurried to the door.

"Hey, I—"

She didn't wait for his explanation; she burst in, pushing past him in a halo of that citrus smell that kicked him right in the chest.

"Really? We're going back to the messy Blake? I was just here. What the heck happened?"

She motioned to all the papers on the floor. Dozens of them. He'd gone through half of a pad trying to get the words right last night. They started out well enough, but the minute he started thinking about what he was doing, the doubt crept in and the words got crappy.

"I've got it under control, okay, clean freak?"

She turned on him then, her eyes searching his for something. "You're late. I had to take that whole tour myself."

He rubbed a hand through his hair, putting his arm down when he smelled himself. "My alarm must not have gone off. I'm sorry."

She stepped closer, her face intent. "You just slept in?"

He nodded. "Yeah. Never done that before?"

Charcoal rimmed eyes narrowed on him, but she seemed to be satisfied by her intense once over. She also seemed to notice his lack of shirt and her eyes shifted to the ground. He hoped she wouldn't catch sight of the handwriting scribbled on the pages on the floor. Yeah ... she noticed.

He watched her dip down, the light seeming to find her wherever she went and casting her in a pool of sunshine. She gathered up a few crumpled sheets and smoothed them out. As soon as Cody realized what she was doing, he hurried over, lunging when she held the pages out of his reach.

"What is this?"

"Nothing. Journey, come on."

"No." She put a hand on his chest, and knowing that he wasn't smelling quite as fresh as he liked, he resisted the urge to reach for the page when he knew he could easily take it. He battled between letting her see what he'd been writing and grossing her out with his B.O.

"This is writing."

"Brilliant. This one gets a gold star," he said, folding his arms over his chest.

"Can I read it?"

"Nope." He managed to snatch the papers from her hand without wafting too much underarm stench.

Her smile was huge, her eyes positively sparkling with delight at the development. "Okay, fine. But promise me this: when you get it hammered out, I get to hear it."

"You're probably the only one who will want to," he assured her.

"No." Journey got closer. Her hand reached out, almost touching his chest before she must have realized what she was doing and snatched it back. "That's where you're wrong. If I, a twenty-something professional, want meaningful, fun, country music with heart, then there are a whole lot of others who feel the same."

He shook his head. He wasn't quite sure he believed her, but something inside of him wanted to more than he was ready to admit.

"Come on, Sleepy. We've got an ATV tour in twenty minutes, and you smell like Bigfoot drank skunk juice. Clean up. I'll grab some breakfast-to-go from Ruby and meet you in the barn."

That sounded way more promising than he knew it would be. And when did he start wanting to corner Journey Miller in the barn? He shook that idea right out of his head and hurried to the shower.

෨✼✼✼ଓ

Journey walked into the gathering room a few days later, weaving her way between tables filled with guests who were up early for excursions. They were drinking coffee and indulging in the inn's iconic cinnamon rolls. Stepping next to the bar that ran the length of the kitchen counter, Journey peered over it, looking for Ruby. They surprised each other when Ruby popped up, her hat askew and her normally cheerful manner bubbling with panic.

"Oh, Journey. I'm so glad to see you! It's an emergency of epic proportions!" Ruby motioned for Journey to follow her through the swinging doors into the kitchen where a large island dominated the room. When they were inside, Journey braced herself for something horrible and pressed Ruby to begin.

"What is it, Rubes?"

"Oh! I knew I should never have come up with that idea. This is why I need an assistant. Breakfast for dinner; who does that? Do you know who? Crazy people who haven't slept because they've been drinking too much coffee while making their cinnamon rolls. *Those* are the kinds of people who come up with these ideas. Omelets for dinner. What do you think we need for omelets, Journey?"

Journey blinked, still waiting for the emergency. Her brain slowly kicked in. "Um, peppers, mushrooms …" Ruby made continuing motions with her hands, urging her on. "Eggs—"

"That!" She almost yelled it, and Journey's head snapped back. "Eggs." Ruby nearly sobbed. "And where do I get eggs, you might ask?"

Journey nodded as though this may have been her next question also.

"From the farm down the mountain. So convenient. Such fresh, beautiful, colorful eggs. Only, last week, when I went to collect them, that hen *looked* at me, and I swear, I knew!"

"Knew?" Journey was having a hard time following Ruby as she walked around the kitchen, gathering a tray of cinnamon rolls covered in rich cream cheese frosting in each hand.

"I knew I saw it in her beady little chicken eye. That *look w*hen I asked the farmer for 12 dozen more eggs for our omelet night. She's the top chick, like in the mafia. She called a halt. He's completely dry. I'm eggless on omelet night, Journey!" Ruby pushed out of the kitchen, and Journey followed, holding the door open and trying very hard not to laugh.

"Called a halt? Can birds ... do that?"

"They can do anything. Was I being greedy? I don't even know what to think now." Ruby sniffed as she plated up a pan of rolls. "And what do I do now? I can't even make pancake batter. Our first breakfast for dinner is going to be a complete catastrophe."

"There have to be other places to get eggs," Journey said, carefully.

Ruby shook her head. "I can't get store-bought once I've established a farm-fresh kitchen. It would be a total affront to our guests."

Journey touched Ruby's arm gently. "Rubes, I'm sure most of our guests don't even know they're farm fresh eggs."

Ruby looked insulted. "You can't seriously be suggesting I go down to the local market and get three-week-old eggs to serve on omelet night."

"No, I would never suggest that," Journey's face scrunched with uncertainty, "but there has to be a solution. Maybe ... another farmer nearby, a farmer's market, a—"

"That's it!" Ruby snapped, and grabbed Journey's hand. "You're a genius!" She kissed Journey on the cheek, spun into the kitchen, and then returned looking dejected again only seconds later.

"What?"

"I can't go. It's an hour drive to the nearest farmer's market, and I have too much to do here to leave for the morning."

"Well, then this is your lucky day. I just happen to have the day off, and I've been meaning to pay you back for that lemon bread a few weeks ago. This is my chance."

"You have to take someone with you."

"I do?"

Ruby nodded. "That many eggs are a recipe for disaster in a moving vehicle. You need someone in the back seat to hold onto them."

Journey rolled her eyes when Ruby wasn't looking. "Ruby, I think I can handle a few dozen eggs on my own."

But Ruby was already casting around the room. And who happened to walk in just as she was fishing for a companion?

"Cody! There you are. Perfect. You'll go with Journey, right?"

Cody Blake looked better rested than he had in weeks. Even the haunted black circles under his eyes were starting to disappear. "Go where?"

"Rubes, I don't think he can just pick up and leave the inn," Journey said. She whispered, "Probation," into Ruby's ear as quietly as she could.

"Just have to check it out with Mama Lucille or Big Ben is all," Cody said, coming closer and smelling like he had just showered in a waterfall of manliness. Why did he have to smell so good?

Journey turned to him with a forced smile. "But it's your first day off in weeks. I'm sure you'd like to spend it doing something other than an egg run."

"Look, if Ruby needs eggs, I'm in. Besides, I could use some different scenery." Cody was all too helpful, and Journey found herself regretting her morning chore already. Big Ben walked in just then, an enormous cup of coffee in his hand, baseball cap on his head, ready to lead out for the day's events.

"Oh, Ben," Ruby motioned him over, "Cody wanted to run something past ya."

And within moments, everything was approved. Journey was placed in the driver's seat of the inn's Jeep, and Cody was beside her with Ruby giving instructions through the driver's window.

"Look for colored eggs. They're fresher if you shake them and listen *really* close and there's no sloshing. Sloshing is bad! And don't just get brown. We're equal opportunity here. Blue, green, brown, even some white."

"Ruby, I've got this completely under control. You go back and chop veggies to your heart's content. We'll be back after lunch."

"Okay," Ruby looked like she was near tears again, "you're the best, Journey. Thanks, Cody!"

It was a quiet beginning. There was absolutely no radio reception up in the mountains, and Journey wasn't sure where to start.

"I have an iPod," she offered. "We could share the headphones."

Cody shrugged. "Or we could just talk."

Journey smirked. "Us, talk? I don't think we've broached that uncharted territory just yet."

The sun shone in on them at the next turn, prompting an adjustment of visors and sunglasses. And silence. "What if I promise not to assume we're friends, no matter how heart-to-heart this little road trip gets."

"I can still call you a jerk?" Journey was being sarcastic, but just broaching the subject really did make her feel so much better. She wasn't quite ready to give up the safety of her disdain for Cody Blake and all he stood for.

"Knock yourself out." Cody grinned at her and she felt something in her chest that made her focus back on the road. It wasn't helping that he had on a pair of jeans and a button up that looked amazing on him. Not the superstar I'm - ready - to - rock – your - world - with - my - hotness amazing but the regular guy looking - really - great amazing.

She thought about offering to cut his hair. That would be the perfect final touch. Instead, she pressed her lips together, refusing to linger on the thought of running her fingers through his dark curls. Another pool of silence stretched in front of them, interrupted only by the purr of the engine as they climbed the mountain road and then descended on the other side.

"I grew up in North Carolina," Cody said, finally. And then waited.

Journey grimaced. She quickly thought through her early history, wondering where she should begin without giving anything away. Not many people knew about her time in Gunlock. Maybe she could start there, where it was important.

He turned in his seat, his intense blue eye focused on her. She tried not to squirm or wonder if she should have done more than scrunch her dark hair with mousse to bring out the waves and let it fall around her shoulders.

"I'm guessing Minnesota."

"I don't even have an accent," Journey smirked. "I'm from Gunlock, a tiny little town where my grandma lived."

"Lived?"

"Yeah." Journey tried on a smile with the news. Nope. It never got easier. "She passed on three years ago. They sold the house and land."

"Dang, I'm sorry."

"It's fine." Journey turned down a mountain road, following the sign toward Strawberry Creek.

"How about your family?" Cody asked. Journey flexed both hands reflexively on the steering wheel trying not to let the tension she felt show. It wasn't easy to talk about her family. She schooled her voice to be free of emotion.

"Two sisters, Mom, and her husband." She shrugged.

"I take it you're not close." Cody's eyes didn't leave her face.

"Not terribly. Well, that's not true. My middle sister and I are close. Her baby girl is incredible. I could sustain myself on her fresh baby smell alone. I miss her every single day. It's just my mom and older sister. I spent about eight years of my growing-up with my grandma, and we were a perfect match. She was the kind of person who just makes you feel like you can do anything."

"Why did you live with your grandma?"

Despite her best efforts to keep her emotions neutral, Journey felt her shoulders working up again. She worked to relax them. She was grateful she didn't have to look in his eyes when she told this part of her story. It always made her feel like Little Orphan Annie, unwanted and unloved, no matter how her grandma made up for it in the end.

"I got appendicitis the year before I turned twelve." She peeked quickly his way before focusing back on the road. The way his attention was riveted on her did little to still her emotions. "My mom was never really the nurturing type. I guess we had the least in common out of the girls. My older sisters were more her style, and I guess I was just ... different. I loved to sing. I loved to read. I don't know. Disappearing was my thing. Laying low. And everyone was fine with it.

"That ER trip kind of threw me into the spotlight, and the timing could not have been worse. My oldest sister was doing her first pageant, my second sister was already busy with her dreams, and here I was, throwing a wrench in the works. I think that's how it got so bad. I just ... didn't tell anyone I was in pain until I was literally throwing up."

"Woah, that's intense." Journey caught his grimace from a side glance. He was watching her intently and she had to remember to drop the names and details from her story.

"Not the best summer ever," Journey admitted. "I spent a week in the hospital after emergency surgery. They left a hole in me to get all the infection out, a little at a time. On the day I was released, I got into our family SUV, laid down, and woke up six hours later in Gunlock."

"You didn't know?"

Journey shook her head. "We hadn't seen each other since the great Christmas debacle when I was six, and Mom thought I should know the truth about Santa while Grandma was adamantly opposed. Six years later, we were all different people. I had no idea I was going to spend the rest of my recouping time there in that little town. But I guess Mom just didn't have time to be my nurse."

The look of shock on Cody's face made her feel funny inside. She hadn't expected this tender side to show up so easily.

"Man, that sucks."

"It did at first," Journey agreed, "but then it didn't. Grandma was ... everything my mom wasn't. Sometimes I still can't reconcile that Grandma June was my mom's mother. How is that even possible? How can one person be so loving, giving, and wise, and the other so completely self-absorbed and neglectful?"

She shook her head, rolling her shoulders back with a deep inhale. It helped. She tried a grin. "But enough about my pitiful beginnings. What about your family?"

"Four boys, believe it or not," Cody chuckled, running a hand through his thick hair. "I'm the youngest and definitely got in trouble the most. My big brothers are all college grads. One works on the farm back home with Mom and my step dad, and the others are businessmen in the city nearby. I've got a few nieces and nephews. I think I probably had a charmed life growing up.

"My dad dying when I was sixteen from cancer was the first black cloud in my life. It hit me pretty hard. I poured myself into my music, worked hard during the summer to get a demo cut, and then, after my senior year, I headed to Nashville."

"Was that part of your first album?"

"Well," Cody grinned, "no. I was okay at best in the song writing department. I did a lot of hard work honing that skill before I could even get an agent. When I did, my first album was still nothing to write home about. I didn't realize how many steps come before success, you know? A lot of construction work in between gigs. I met my current agent at a talent search night. He was looking for a certain face, and his sales pitch was on point. He convinced me I was it."

Journey gave him a long look before turning back to the road. She could see it there. The shades of regret and chagrin at his mistakes. "That was what got you noticed."

He nodded. "That's when everything changed. Cody Blake became the bad boy of country, breaking barriers, making girls swoon, generally stirring up trouble. From day one, they wanted nothing to do with the music I wrote. I brought some of my songs to the table during our first meeting, and they just put them aside and said if I trusted them, they would have me on every station in the country."

"They made good, didn't they?" Journey's tone was wry. "It's always the same story. Change everything about who you are, be who we want you to be, and you'll get everything you want. They don't realize you wanted something different all along." Journey was telling her own story there, but didn't dare share more.

"Yeah, they don't tell you the dark side of the business or how easy it is to lose your focus." He looked out the window this time. She could see his jaw working, feel him deciding whether to go on. The silence between them was broken when he continued.

"They don't tell you how confusing it is to have women tell you everything you want to hear. Suddenly, everything you know about yourself slips away in the face of abject adoration. I shouldn't tell you this, because heaven knows you don't need encouragement, but I swear, that first day when you treated me like a piece of crap, it was the first time in years that someone was real with me. Other than Ian. He's always been real, and looking back, I regret so much about how I've treated him.

"But the girls. Man. They don't tell you no. Ever. Even when you want them to. And then you stop wanting them to and you forget," he brushed a hand over his face, "everything your mama taught you about how to treat a girl, what your dad preached about showing respect. It's this selective amnesia, because you know damn well you'll reckon for it someday, but it feels like that day will never come."

He paused, and she knew he was showing her something of his soul he hadn't shown anyone in a long time. Saying things he hadn't said out loud before. Realizations were popping up where there had been clouds and excuses before. He breathed out a sigh that sounded heavy with remorse, and something in her ached for him. She knew what that sigh felt like.

"Okay, I'm going to go all philosophical on you for a minute, so just hang tight. My grandma always said that we all make mistakes. *'Mistakes are a part of life.'* That was her mantra. And then she would follow up with, *'It's not how many times you fall down, it's what you do while you're down there and how quick you get back up.'* She told me that some people think there is no hope. Once you're down, you're down for good. Some people like to wallow in their wretchedness. And then, some people just shake it off and try again. And here's the last one, and then I'm done. *'Only you can decide how long you stay down. No one can force you to get up and start running the race again. You have to choose to forgive yourself and move on.'* "

Cody shifted in his seat again and studied her.

"Too much?"

He shook his head. "Just makes me wish I could have met her. Man, she must have been a force to be reckoned with."

Journey smiled. "She was everything to me. I can't believe life had the balls to go on without her."

"Yeah, tell me about it. That's exactly how I felt when my dad died."

It was just then that the sign for Strawberry Fields Farmer's Market came into view, and Journey turned them into the small parking lot beside a bunch of colorful pop-up tents.

They got out of the Jeep, and Cody walked over, his sunglasses shielding his expression. "Wanna just … I don't know … pretend we're friends while we're here?"

"I thought we had an understanding," Journey hedged. Something about getting close to Cody felt dangerous. Like dangling your bleeding heart above a swarm of hungry sharks. Blood would be spilt.

"And I'm cool with that. Just thought we could try it out."

She snuck a look at him and saw the hope etched in his brow and in the way he stood.

"Sure. But just for this. When we get back …"

"Exactly. Everything's back to normal."

She nodded, took a deep breath, and smiled at him. "Shall we get some eggs?"

ಬ✾✾✾ಜ

Before they could get eggs, they had to wander the market, musing over the wares and chatting with a variety of salespeople. One woman was selling hand knitted animal clothing. Cats, dogs, goats, and chickens could wear her specialty items. Cody and Journey chuckled over the image of a chicken in a knitted tux.

Cody was drawn to a stand with roasted and candied nuts. The rich aroma was enticing. After one crunchy handful, he bought himself a bag to share with Journey on the way back to the inn. They collected cartons of fresh strawberries, a ripe cantaloupe, and a basket of peaches. Journey got a tray of fudge to take to

Mama Lucille and a bag of chocolate nut clusters for Ruby.

It turned out that eggs were easy to come by at this little outdoor market. Max McKee was at the end table, and his tent was filled with eggs. Twelve dozen made a dent, though, and he was kind enough to fill the large egg crates with a mixture from his variety of hues and sizes.

"These ones come from my Bantams. And these are Araucana eggs. Give you that greenish blue color every time." Max was a tall man with bright blue eyes, a well-groomed white goatee and a cowboy hat that tipped respectfully when they approached his stand.

"These are excellent," Journey felt proud of herself, "and we'll take an extra dozen just in case."

"You coming from Snowflake Falls Inn?" Max looked through his glasses at them as he transferred eggs.

"Yes we are," Cody nodded, "sent on a special mission for farm fresh eggs."

"Won't find many fresher. My hens are free range too, which means they're a happy bunch. Have some goose and duck eggs if you need 'em. We support the hatching programs in the schools nearby, taking in the newly hatched chicks and giving them a home."

"Oh, we hatched eggs at my grandma's one spring. I think a baby chick is probably the softest thing I've ever held. They grew up to be feisty hens, that's for sure. But there's something neat about raising them up from eggs," Journey said.

"Sounds like your sweetheart is going to want some chickens soon, cowboy." Max winked, stacking the final crate on top.

Cody smiled broadly at his reference. "Yes it does," he agreed.

Journey shot him a look that would have killed chickens and smiled back at Max. "Thanks, Max. These are literally saving omelet night. We'll make sure to spread the word about your stand."

"Much obliged." Max tipped his hat again. "Need a hand loading these up?"

They both refused his help, grabbing six and seven crates respectively. At the Jeep, they loaded the crates carefully into the back seat.

"Want to stop for lunch somewhere?" Cody managed to wedge himself into the seat beside the eggs to keep watch over them.

"Did you see a place?"

"Just a little diner off the highway, maybe five miles back toward the inn."

They pulled off a little later at the diner. It was a cozy place with only a smattering of tables. Once seated, they noticed that the same man who took the orders ended up grilling them.

They found a booth and both chose burgers from the laminated menus.

"Want to share a shake when we're done?" Cody asked, turning to her and pointing out a glossy picture of a shake topped with whipped cream and bright red cherry. It looked tasty.

"It depends. What kind of sharing do you do? You get three sips, and I get one?"

"Wow, I sense some distrust." Cody leaned in. "Where is this coming from, Journey. I'm really hurt."

Journey slapped his arm. "Oh, please. I had a boyfriend in high school. I established early on that there was no sharing drinks or ice cream with him. I would get one swig and then the cup would be empty. One bite of ice cream, and he would finish off the bowl while I was trying not to get a brain freeze."

"Ah, high school boyfriends can be lame."

"Yeah," she laughed, "so just give it to me straight. Can I trust you to share, or should we just cut our losses and each get a shake?"

Cody leaned forward, taking her hand and looking into her eyes with an intensity that caught her attention. "Journey, I promise to share with you. I'll even let you have the last slurp if you like."

She grinned, and shook his hand. "I like the sound of that. Just don't blow it. My general trust in sharing dairy products with a man is in your hands."

Their lunch was actually fun. They laughed more than Cody thought was possible. He told her funny stories about growing up on his parent's farm with three older brothers. She dunked fries in fry sauce, and looked like she might want to lick the small plastic bowl it came in. They got their shake and shared it on the way back to the inn, passing it back and forth with a pair of straws. He made good on his promise and let her have the last slurp of chocolaty goodness.

A short time later, Journey carefully pulled into the dirt near the side door of the inn and stepped out of the Jeep. She met Cody who straightened his shirt and pulled his sunglasses off. The sunshine was still bright, but here, near the inn, it was diffused by a copse of trees with long full branches stretching to shade the earth.

He started to say something, but she stopped him with her hand on his arm—something she quickly removed, though the warmth of her fingerprints still sank into his skin.

"Thanks for not being a jerk."

He grinned, grateful for the way she put them back at ease with just one well-placed jab.

"Yeah, it was hard, but somehow, I pulled it off."

She looked away and then up at him through thick, dark lashes. His first instinct in that moment was to give in to the growing desire in his chest to tip her face toward his and capture her lips with his own. He'd spent more time than he cared to admit admiring that mouth, even when it was telling him things he didn't want to hear. But she was already moving away, and he knew the timing was still terribly off.

"Want to help me with these eggs? I'm sure Ruby will reward us with something tasty."

"Sure." Cody grabbed his stack of crates and followed her into the inn. The entire time, he was wondering how in the world this nightmare of a community service gig could have turned into one of the best times he'd had in years.

"Ian, it's me, Cody." It felt weird to start out the call like that, but it had been a while since he'd called his friend just to talk—or in this case, to apologize. He was standing in the middle of the meadow, where the best reception happened to come in. There was something about the openings in the trees and the curve of the mountain that made it a haven for cell phone use. This was where Lucille stood to call her daughter once a week.

It had been over a week since that day at the Farmer's market when Journey quoted her Grandma June about getting up after falling down. Since then, Cody had felt a growing unease with how he'd handled this particular fall. Not only had he been a complete jerk to his best friend at his sentencing, he'd been blowing him off for months before that.

Looking back, the council of his sensible, caring friend rang with greater clarity than ever before. It was something he would have drank away had he been drinking. Something he would have easily let sink into the background of his already screaming conscience before, but now, with no alcohol to muddle the memories, everything was coming back sharp and clear. With this dawning came a heaping dose of mortification. The only way he could think to get it off his mind was to face it, even though that promised even more embarrassment.

"Hey, Cody. Is there something wrong?" The unease in his voice came through loud and clear, and Cody kicked himself again for becoming that kind of friend.

"Yeah, there's ... just something I needed to talk to you about. Do you have a minute?"

"That's why you pay me the big bucks," Ian said, irony lacing his voice. Cody seemed to recall hurling that accusation at him several times during their last meeting. Now, he grimaced. "Ian, I'm not really sure how to do this, so I'm just diving in."

The apology was awkward and painful, as admitting weaknesses can be. But Ian was incredibly willing to accept it.

"Cody, I mean it. I forgive you, man. You just don't know how happy I am to hear you say that."

Cody laughed a little. "Yeah. I can't believe it took me this long. Dude, I totally owe you, so keep that in mind. If there's anything I can do when this is all cleared up, you let me know."

"Yeah," Ian paused, "I appreciate that, Cody, I really do. But friendship isn't about evening scores or paybacks. Yeah, the last couple years have really sucked, but we're cool. You being in this place where you can make some amends, that's payback for me. I love you like a brother, man. Seeing you go through this, thinking I might lose you ... that's the hardest thing I've ever done. So, you don't have to pay me back or comp me out. You just live a good life, and we're even. I know there'll be a day when I need you to be there for me."

Cody couldn't speak for a moment. Ian's unexpected kindness had shoved a rock of emotion into his throat, and all he could do was make listening noises until he finally worked his way around it.

"Ian, you're legit. Thank you."

※※※

Journey felt restless, possibly a result of overindulging in Ruby's chocolate croissants hours earlier, and possibly a consequence of ignoring the ever-growing feeling in her chest every time she spent time with Cody. Their drive together on the great egg rescue of the year hadn't helped. The frozen barrier she'd constructed between the two of them felt like it was melting under the hot summer sun. Fast, furious, and refreshing.

She wanted to walk over and invent a reason to hang out with him, but that was getting a little too predictable. How often could she show up at his cabin late at night before it started to look wrong?

Instead of stopping at his cabin, she went further to the kitchen where Ruby was putting her delicious cinnamon rolls to bed in the fridge for the night. The new assistant she'd been interviewing was starting the next morning, and she wanted everything in place.

"Watcha doing, Journey?"

Journey shrugged and then jumped up and down in one place.

"Cabin fever?"

Journey snapped. "Yes! That's it. I can't ... I need to *do* something."

Ruby nodded, unbuttoning her chef's coat and hanging it on the hook with a yawn. "I know just what you mean. My sisters and I would always get this way at the end of our visits to Lake Tahoe. We had this gorgeous cabin and went boating all day, but it was the nights, when there was no reception and only cousins as far as the eye could see, that we felt ready to tear the house apart."

"Well, that's definitely not an option," Journey said, looking over her shoulder into the gathering room where a large contingent of university cheerleaders had gathered for a movie. The white screen glowed down on the group, some of whom looked like they were feeling cabin fever too and had moved to the outside of the group to talk and giggle.

"I've got it," Journey said, turning to Ruby with glowing brown eyes. "Emergency Dance Party!"

"Dancing?" Ruby was slipping into her hoodie and fighting the zipper. "But where?"

"I've got speakers, a great playlist ..."

"And a cabin the size of a postage stamp?"

Journey squared her shoulders. "It would just be us, maybe some of those cheerleaders, and ..."

"Please say Cody, please say Cody." Ruby clasped her hands prayer like and chanted the words.

"Fine, but you have to invite him, because I'm not."

A hand on her hip. "Don't tell me you're still not friends."

"We're not. I don't hate him, but don't get crazy on me." Journey tossed this over her shoulder while striding toward the girls on the fringe. There were five of them and a couple of guys who were probably cheerleaders too. The invitation was well received. Within moments, Journey was hooking up her music player to the portable speakers and moving all the furniture in her cabin living area up against the walls and into the small kitchen space. Once the music started, people appeared. The lights were reduced to collections of candles placed carefully around the room, out of the reach of dancing bodies.

There was something incredibly infectious about music blasting into the night. The door remained open, pouring in the cool mountain air and letting the group grow larger as it trickled out onto the porch.

Journey was in the middle of it all, bouncing to the rhythm, forgetting everything but the feel of the music. Ruby was right there with her, laughing and dancing, leaning in to shout over the bass. "I can't believe how good it feels to dance after a long day. We should make this a regular thing."

Journey grinned and agreed. Yes. There was something about music that set her free. She joined the others around her, jumping during the lyrics of a particularly fun song.

Journey didn't notice that Ruby was gone for a few minutes, but when she looked around, there she was, just coming in the door, bobbing her way through a dozen bodies. Right behind her was Cody Blake, looking freshly showered and even better than he had the last time she saw him. Was that even possible? Journey wasn't the only one who noticed. She heard a few appreciative whispers from the ladies in the room and knew Ruby's addition to the crowd was much appreciated.

"What is this?" Cody asked Journey the moment they reached her.

She looked around like his question was obvious. Leaning in to be heard over the thump of the music, she said, "Emergency Dance Party, Blake. Can't ya tell?"

"She was getting cabin fever," Ruby yelled.

Cody caught her gaze and grinned. "Why am I not surprised? Who are all these people?"

He looked around at all the dancing bodies and giggling smiles.

"Cheerleader group from the University. We're taking them up to the bridge tomorrow. You're welcome."

ಜಿ❄❄❄ಲ

Cody took in the crowd around him that felt bigger than it was in these tight quarters. But nothing quite captured his attention like watching Journey. He didn't know how she did it, how she made living her life look so effortless and passionate. For a long moment, he watched her lean into the music, close her eyes and just dance. He'd be lying if he said she wasn't incredible. There were people all around her, way more than should legally be allowed in such a small space. But no one seemed to mind. And she didn't either.

He studied the room, moving a little to the music as he did so. What he found surprised him. These girls were Tiffany clones. Lots of girls with great hair, beautiful long legs, coy looks in his direction, and moves that suggested they were willing to like him on sight. And yet, the pull he felt toward them didn't show up like it had before. He talked to a few of the girls who approached him; he heard them laugh at his jokes, and he could only smile, because his eyes kept finding their way back to the little brunette in the middle of the room. Her hair fell into her face; she was belting the lyrics and then pumping her fist in the air. She and Ruby were like sisters, laughing and singing along.

There weren't many slow songs on this playlist, but when one popped up, and Journey took Ruby's hand, he knew he had to do something. Maybe he should have asked one of the cute blonds flirting with him, but what he really wanted was a reason to be close to the girl in the middle of the room.

Carefully weaving his way through the crush of bodies, he was able to reach her elbow. She turned from the guy she was talking to and lifted her brow.

"Want to dance?"

She looked doubtful. "Not a lot of room for the waltz in here, cowboy."

"Yeah, I noticed," he said, tugging her closer. There may not have been a lot of space, but there was definitely room for what he was thinking of. A hand at her waist and the other cupping her tiny palm in his, he moved her in a very, very small two-step.

"Emergency Dance Party, huh?"

She tipped her head up to look into his face, meeting his gaze with her dark warm eyes. "Sometimes you just have to dance."

"You look like you're having fun."

She grinned. "Music does it for me."

"I'm getting that feeling."

A couple cheerleaders moved past them, and he used it as an excuse to slip his hand further around her back. Her waist was small enough to allow him to easily wrap his arm around her, closing the distance between them. It was a brilliant move he did not regret for a moment, because it moved her hand up his shoulder until it cupped the back of his neck. There was something about her fingertips messing with his too-long hair that made his heart race.

When she rocked up on her tiptoes to whisper in his ear, he thought he might have a heart attack.

"You need a haircut, Blake." For once, he couldn't argue. His overlong hair had become less a style choice and more a byproduct of missing his stylist for six months.

"Know anyone who could make it happen?"

"Got some scissors in my bathroom," she said. Now they were getting somewhere. The thought of having her hands in his hair was one he did not mind entertaining. She tugged at his hand.

"Right now?"

"I can't really handle your shagginess much longer," Journey tossed over her shoulder. She came out of her bathroom with a pair of scissors and then lead him out on the back porch, flipping on a light to compliment the work being done by the moon in a cloudless sky. They settled for a patio chair and towel to keep him hair free.

"All right, I'm not promising runway quality, but I can trim you up," she said, running her hands through his soft dark curls. He eyes slid closed while listening to her voice and the sound of scissors and hair crossing paths. He interrupted the steady snip of the scissors with his question.

"How did you learn to cut hair?"

There was a slight pause where she tipped his head to one side and he felt the cold of metal against his skin while she trimmed the curls at his neck.

"I have two sisters who are ridiculously fashionable. They change their style on the slightest whim, and I was the one they made watch a bunch of boring YouTube videos to make it happen. Believe me, I've butchered some hairdos, mostly their Barbies, but I finally got pretty good at it. Until I left—then they found a real stylist."

She worked her way around his head, measuring and cutting. "Good grief, your hair is thick and soft, just like your lashes. Long, thick, every girl's dream. Why heaven wastes great lashes on boys is a question I will be happy to ask the good Lord when I see Him next."

Cody grinned. "Are you saying I have nice hair?"

"I'm saying," she used her hand to tilt his chin so that he was looking up into her face rimmed in moonlight, "you're not bad looking if you try not to be a jerk about it."

"You think I'm hot." He nodded his head in appreciation.

She snipped the scissors in the air. "Reign it in, cocky, or I'll leave you with a bald spot to bring you some humility."

He grinned up at her and gave in to the urge. His hands reached out, cupping her hips and tugging her between his knees. She was short enough that, even from his seated position, he didn't have to tilt his head far to look into her eyes. They were pools of blackness in the dark.

"You never say what I think you will, Journey."

She'd steadied herself with both hands on his shoulders. "It's a gift." Her words came out in a whisper that gave him courage. For once, she wasn't pushing him away. There was something tempting about the way her hair collected around her cheeks when she looked down into his face. The electricity he felt from the warmth of her hands and the look in her eyes told him that if he asked, she would say yes.

"I really want to kiss you right now," he said, urging her even closer, the sides of his thighs brushing against hers and his hands moving up from her hips to her back. Her lips were inches from his when they heard the music stop and Ruby's nervous laugh, followed by her voice from inside the house. "Journey?"

Chapter Seven

Journey pulled back with a jerk, her head spinning. There were scissors in her hand and hands on her hips that completely sucked her brain dry of all rational thought. She blew out a quick breath and looked around, the sudden silence bringing her back to the moment.

Oh, yeah. Dance party. Lots of people crammed into her little cabin. She grabbed her phone from her back pocket. Oh, no. What was supposed to be an hour-long diversion had wound it's way dangerously close to midnight.

"Uh oh." Journey cast one regretful glance back at Cody —who was shaking off any loose hair and standing to follow her—as she rounded the cabin to find Lucille standing on the front porch with a lantern in her hand. She was in her pajamas, and her face was less annoyed than it was curious.

"What's going on here, Journey? I heard loud music and thought it was comin' from the gathering room. When I went to check, everything was closed up for the night."

"Emergency Dance Party?" The end of Journey's answer turned it up into a question. Was she busted?

"There are 22 people in your cabin," Lucille said after looking around, "and I can hear the music from inside the inn."

"Yeah, um … we invited some of the cheerleaders, and then a few other guests must have heard … I'm so sorry."

Ruby pushed her way to the porch while several couples melted into the darkness on their way back to the inn. Lucille looked around for a moment before turning back to Journey.

"Maybe we should revisit this in the mornin'?"

Journey nodded, smiling brightly at the remaining guests. "Yes, ma'am." She turned to whoever was left. "That's all the fun for tonight, folks. Thanks for coming!"

As the group filtered away, Lucille cast one last glance at the trio standing in the twinkling light of Journey's porch before following the others into the inn.

"Oy! I feel like I just got busted by my mom." Journey breathed out a sigh of relief. That could have gone so much worse.

"Thank goodness there were no boys in the bathroom." Ruby added, double taking when they both looked at her with raised brows. "What? It happened once, and let me tell you, making out in the loo is not as glamorous as they lead you to believe."

That was enough. Journey looked at Cody, and they couldn't help but dissolve into laughter.

"Oh, hey! You got your hair cut." Ruby said. It only made them laugh harder. When they'd all reigned in their giggles, Journey sighed as she walked through her front door. The candles went out with a puff of air over each flame. Ruby and Cody started moving the couch, chair, and table back into place around the room.

"That goes there. Thanks, guys. Hey, at least we rocked out, right?" Journey was feeling the day and the call of her very comfortable bed.

"That was the most fun I've had in a long time," Cody agreed.

They all grinned at each other, and Ruby seemed to notice the heat between Journey and Cody, because she stopped grinning and backed away. "Well, I'm going to go get some sleep. Those cinnamon rolls don't cook themselves, y'know?"

"G'night, Ruby," Journey called.

Journey stifled a yawn. "I'm so tired. Finally. Guess I'll see you tomorrow."

"Yeah," he said, hesitating on the threshold. The look on his face said he wasn't tired as much as wishing there was a way to recreate that moment on the back porch. Instead, he edged out the door. "Night."

"Night." Journey wiggled her fingers at him, giggling when he forgot the step off the porch and then recovered. Slowly, she pushed the door closed, flicking off the lights once again, and took a three-step-leap approach to the bed. She was deeply grateful for the heaviness of her lids, and the pull of her warm mattress, because there was no other way she could stop thinking about Cody Blake, superstar.

ಸಂ✻✻✻ಲ

The mountains were in high spirits the next morning, sheltered in a fog when the day began that quickly burned away under bright sunshine. Birds called to one another. The resident woodpecker tap-tap-tapped away with his mysterious Morse code messages at a trunk nearby. Journey always thought it a good omen to have him around, doing his thing. She was halfway up the trail toward the bridge with a herd of cheerleaders. They were a bouncy group with a lot of bright laughter and loud calls to one another. It reminded her of her days at Pine View High.

The sunshine drenching her with it's bright joyfulness and heavenly warmth made up for the murky beginning. Mornings on the mountain always started out with a breath of chill that had her zipping up her hoodie and wishing she'd brought gloves. Even with the extra layer she had happily packed on since coming to Snowflake Falls, and all of Ruby's irresistible cooking, she still shivered easier than most. It only took a brisk walk and tipping her head up to the sunshine to get warmed up.

She watched Cody up ahead as he lead the peppy crowd. Most of the ladies were flirting madly with Cody while they traipsed along the dirt trails. Each path was fringed in wildflowers stretching their petals toward the sky.

Journey tried not to let herself think of the night before, of the feel of his hands on her hips, or the rush of heat in her abdomen when he pulled her closer, his lips so close to hers she could still feel the warmth of his nearness this morning. A deep breath and a shake out of her shoulders got her mind off that and on the trail ahead.

She answered a few questions for the coaches and pointed out the nearby meadow where they could execute their team building exercises while still enjoying the photo opportunities on the bridge.

The coaches called out, breaking up the flirt-athon with their guide and gathering their team among the grass and wildflowers.

Journey continued on silently, wishing the bridge was all her own this morning. She could use a good talk with Grandma to get her thoughts organized. Almost kissing Cody had unlocked some of her deep-set fears, and now she wasn't sure she was on the right track. Reaching the bridge, she unzipped her hoodie—warmed through by the sun—and wrapped it around her waist.

"Finally warmed up?"

Cody came up right beside her, leaning his back against the bridge railing that she was resting her elbows on.

"Yep." She looked down into the water, loving the sound of it rushing by beneath them.

"Last night," he started to say, and she turned to rest her hip against the railing and get a better look at his face. His hair looked good cleaned up around the edges. She could tell he'd taken time to trim up his beard too, and caught herself glancing at his lips. She wondered what he would say and wondered even more what she *wanted* him to say. "That was a lot of fun."

"Yeah," she nodded, folding her arms across her chest, "and look, your hair didn't turn out half bad."

He nodded with a grin. "Gee, thanks."

"I could do a lot more with some clippers."

"I thought you liked the curls back there." He motioned to the little bit she'd left at the nape of his neck.

"It's not me you've got to impress. If I remember right, you left the world clean-cut and freshly shaved. What are they going to do when you come back looking like this?" She reached out and ran her fingers along his jawline covered in soft, dark scruff.

He shrugged, stepping a bit closer, drawn in by her touch. "Guess I'll worry about that when it gets here."

Journey ignored the flame that ran up her arm after touching his face and looked toward the meadow where girls were taking turns falling backward into each other's waiting arms.

"I remember those days," Journey sighed. Cody's brows rose on his forehead, his smile taking on a teasing quality.

"You were a cheerleader?"

"Heck yeah, I was a cheerleader." She pasted on an overenthusiastic smile and struck a pose, bopping her head forward, one hand on her hip and one fist in the air in the quintessential cheerleader stance.

"I don't know." Cody was studying her closely, a look that almost made her shiver. "I thought cheerleaders were supposed to be pleasant and cheerful."

She smirked. "More like sassy and smart. Besides, I can be cheerful when I want to be."

"Just not around me," he suggested.

Journey's brown eyes searched his face for a minute. "I'm getting better. You can't deny that."

He edged closer. "I definitely can't deny that things have changed."

The urge to close the distance between them was hard to fight, but she knew she had to. Yeah, maybe things had changed between them to a point where she didn't mind spending time with him and might even be wondering what it would feel like to kiss that full lower lip of his, but that didn't alter the facts.

This was a simple detour for him. Within weeks, he would be back to the city, back to his old life and everything that came with it. Kissing him right now might be plenty of fun, but she would pay the price for that fun big time when he went back. Or when he discovered who she really was. Either way, it wouldn't be pretty.

"Journey, I ..."

"You can take it from here, right?" Journey pushed herself off the steel posts.

"Um ... sure?"

"Cool. I just remembered I was supposed to meet with Lucille this morning."

"Okay … yeah. I got this."

She grinned. "Try not to overdose on the eye candy."

He flashed her a thumbs up, but she could feel his gaze as she walked away. For some reason, it was getting harder to do.

༺✵✵༻

A week later, Journey was sitting cross-legged on the barstool, picking through blueberries when she made the announcement.

"Karaoke?" Ruby clapped her hands even though she was holding eggs, and the result was disaster in yolk down her white chef coat. Her assistant, Dante, hid an eye roll as he went back into the kitchen with arms full of bowls.

"Ah, jeez. This was already my third coat this morning. First the thing with the pudding—I mean, that whisk had it out for me—and now this."

"What happened to the second one?" Journey looked up from her blueberries.

Ruby stopped wiping yolk from her tummy and made a face. "Got a little close to the flame."

Journey's eyes widened. "You set yourself on fire?"

Ruby giggled. "Good thing Cody was in here early. That guy is fast with a fire extinguisher." A dimple flashed on her cheek: her tell when she was smitten.

Journey threw a blueberry at Ruby, but she just caught it and popped it in her mouth, disappearing into the back room to grab the mop and a new jacket. She was going to have to start coming in for breakfast earlier if she didn't want to miss the pyrotechnics.

"I was here," Dante called, but Ruby walked back into the room rolling a yellow mop bucket and cast Journey a look before drawing close enough to whisper.

"He's not as fast with an extinguisher. Should have asked him that in the interview."

She started to attack the egg mess. "Tell me more about this karaoke business."

"Well, I talked to Lucille last week about the whole Emergency-Dance-Party thing, and she was pretty impressed with the turnout. Thought maybe we could schedule a bigger one here in the dining room when we have groups like that. I suggested karaoke—"

"Wait … do you sing?" Ruby stopped mopping up gloppy egg whites and pinned Journey with her intense blue eyes.

Journey studied the blueberries more carefully and worked on a casual shrug. "A little, you?"

She thought she pulled it off well enough, because Ruby blew her bangs up in a puff and sighed tragically. "I *want* to sing. I feel it building up inside of me like this." She patted her chest almost like Tarzan, letting the mop handle drop in the process. "Lion ready to roar!" She made the claws of a lion. "But it comes out kind of off-key and whimpery." She looked a little defeated and then brightened. "But I do love music and dancing."

Journey nodded, completely entertained and adoring of her friend. "Yep, found that out the other night."

"Me, too. When's the next dance party?" It was Cody's voice, and Journey turned in her seat to look at him.

"Adding firefighter to your list of redeeming qualities?"

He chuckled. "I do what I can."

"He was *so* amazing." Ruby leaned on the counter, propping her face in her hands and looking with adoration at her hero. "I don't even have a burn." Here, she held up her arm for examination, and Journey stepped down from her stool to check it out.

"You're right. Just singed off your blond hair."

"Oh yeah, I am blond. Forgot about that." She poofed her pink curls under her bandana. She'd added the new hue a week before, totally over her violet tips.

Journey resisted the urge to crack a blond joke in light of the morning's string of disasters. Instead, when Ruby bent down to grab something, Journey pushed a hand under her curls to keep them from sloshing into the eggs that had made it into the bowl in front of her.

"Watcha makin' here, Rubes?"

"Personal quiches. Want one? They are going to be divine. I have an amazing cheese I picked up from the Farmer's market that will take you right to heaven."

"Cheese heaven sounds pretty darn nice," Cody said, and then amended, "though I am a cheddar kind of guy."

Both pairs of eyes turned to him with a look of shock. "Cheddar?"

"You expect me to create heaven with cheddar?" Ruby looked doubtful of her previous good opinion of

Cody. "Cody, I'm not a miracle worker. I can't even make mac and cheese heaven with cheddar alone." She waved him closer. "Just leave it to me. You won't regret this."

And then she was gone, humming, whisking, dropping hand ripped spinach and professionally chopped onions into frothing whipped eggs.

ॐ✼✼✼ॐ

"Wow, cheddar shunning is alive and well in America." Cody crossed his arms and leaned his back on the counter in mock solemnity.

"Just don't mention," Journey leaned closer, and he had a hard time remembering what they were talking about because she smelled really good, "mushrooms."

He nodded with understanding. "I won't." And he wouldn't. He couldn't even recall the word she'd said, because he was still inhaling the smell of her shampoo and forgetting his name. She'd put some distance between them since that night on the back porch, and he was still trying to close it.

"Ruby, I'm going to run to my cabin and grab a sweatshirt. Be right back. Don't give my quiche away."

Ruby waved her off, too content in her creation to pay much attention. She called to Dante for ingredients she'd forgotten. His in-and-out delivery set the swinging door into motion. But that wasn't what had Cody's attention. He watched Journey leave the inn, suppressing the urge to follow her. Humming as she returned in a teal blue hoodie zipped halfway, she slid back onto her barstool and cut a glance in his direction. He tried not to be so obvious about staring at her.

There was something so familiar about her, especially in that blue color. He just could not, for the life of him, put his finger on what it was. He'd spent all night going through the photos on his phone, though the cracked screen made it hard to see clearly. He decided to take a risk and finally blurted it out.

"I feel like I've met you before …"

She cocked an eyebrow at him and smirked. "Nice try, cowboy, but memory loss never looks attractive on a guy."

"I like memory loss," Ruby chirped, before ducking back into the kitchen where she'd tucked the quiches into the oven to bake several minutes before.

He blew out a breath, resisting the urge to step closer to her and examine her eyes. That was where he kept getting hung up. Each time he thought he had a hit, it all dissolved. It was an awards show in Vegas that kept swimming to the top of his memory. But that whole weekend was a total blur. Other than that embarrassing video shot by someone back stage.

"I'm not hitting on you. I'm saying I feel like I've met you before, and I just can't shake it. My luck, you're one of the girls I did wrong in a drunken blur, and you're biding your time before exacting your revenge."

Journey burst out laughing. "Oh, man, you give yourself way too much credit." She pinned him with eyes the color of molten cocoa. It almost took his breath away when she stood up and put her hand on one hip. The scent of her, clean, sassy, and inches from him—literally close enough to touch if he ever got the guts up to try again—washed over him. There was something about her that brought his scattered thoughts into focus.

"Let's be clear, Blake. Even if you 'did me wrong,'" she made air quotes, and even they dripped in contempt, "I would not waste even one precious hour of my life trailing your sorry tail. In fact, I would thank my lucky stars I got out while the gettin' was good. I don't have time for exacting revenge on guys who don't value a girl for more than the way she looks in painted-on jeans and his stinky old T-shirt. Get me?"

Those last words sent his mind to a place where she was wearing his T-shirt, and he had a hard time formulating a reply.

"Gotcha," he managed finally, after an audible swallow.

"What she means is," Ruby amended, bringing three plates around the counter. Each one held a small round ramekin of steaming quiche baked to perfection and a side of freshly cut berries. She placed them on a table next to the pair. Journey had her arms folded and was regarding her friend with a warning in her eyes. Cody was still staring at Journey, trying to shake the urge to touch her hair. "She wants a guy who likes her for more than her cute figure and sassy comebacks."

Cody and Journey looked at each other in amused surprise at the same moment, and suddenly, they were both laughing.

"Ruby …" Journey didn't finish, she just slid into her seat, folding one leg beneath her and picking up a fork. "These look amazing. It is only by the hiking of this mountain day-in and day-out that I can still claim to have a figure."

Cody decided to remain silent on the subject of Journey's body. It still surprised him how attractive he found her with each passing day. The fact that he'd dismissed her with less than a glance during their first encounter still baffled him. But maybe it was too soon to tell her he couldn't stop thinking about her, and her figure was one he could stare at for hours.

Yes, after that set-down moments earlier, he'd better cool his jets. He turned his attention instead to the quiche he was enjoying far more than a country boy should without cheddar. Ruby really was a magician.

"If you're asking my opinion," Ruby tipped her head to the side, "I think your figure has only improved since you got here. Of course, I've never been a fan of super skinny."

Journey was too distracted by her own delicious breakfast to pay much attention to what Ruby was saying. The combination of finely chopped veggies, whipped eggs, and tiny clumps of some kind of cheese made for the gods was overwhelming.

Once again, she wondered why she'd wasted so much time *not* eating. She'd once gone a whole week only drinking lemonade and sucking on hard candies. How the heck had she done that? And why? The reasoning behind her and her sisters' obsession with being super skinny seemed absurd at this point.

Yes, she was not nearly the same size she'd been, but there was something comforting about the way her clothes fit and the way they hugged the body she was coming to know.

"I used to avoid food," Journey admitted, in between sips of orange juice.

Ruby looked at her. "What do you mean *avoid*?" She looked as though the concept had never crossed her mind. "Why on earth would you do that?"

Journey shrugged. "I don't even know now." She ran a hand through her hair and laughed. "At the time, it was so imperative, and now, I can't even think of why that would be a good idea."

Cody studied her. "I once dated a girl who never ate. Not once, the whole time we dated. We would go out to eat, and she drank but never ate one thing. Not even a French fry from my plate. It always made me feel uncomfortable. Like maybe she was a vampire."

Journey rolled her eyes. "She wasn't a vampire, she was just trying to stay skinny so you would like her. It's every girl's dilemma. Keep up the image or be a real human being."

"But I liked her already."

"Why?" Journey leveled dark brown eyes on him and it made him squirm.

He reflected for a minute. "Because she was hot."

"Exactly." Journey snapped her fingers, the sound reverberating in the quiet room. "You liked her *body*. Let me guess, long legs, unnaturally great rack, teeny tiny waist."

Cody blinked. It was like she was reading his mind. "Um … yeah."

Journey leaned forward. "Just so you know, that doesn't usually occur in nature. That body has been dieted, surgically enhanced, and waxed to within an inch of its life. This," she stood up and turned a quick spin, "is your average, everyday girl. A little too much pie to get that thigh gap everyone's crazy about, way too short to qualify for the model crowd. I've gone up two sizes in these jeans, and I sweat every single day. Not exactly the glistening look that most superstars are looking for."

"You're wrong." Cody interrupted her, mainly because if she kept asking him to look at her body, he was going to lose his mind. "Guys like girls who are real, normal, sometimes even sassy."

"No, *you're* wrong." Journey leaned in. "Think through your list of past girlfriends, and tell me one real girl you've dated in the last year alone."

He blew out a breath, running a hand through his hair. She had him. "I was screwed up, okay? I wasn't looking for someone I wanted to settle down with."

"Yeah, but the thing is, every girl who dated you wanted to be the one you thought was good enough to settle down with. Every time you validate their ridiculous regimen by finding them irresistible, the rest of the normal girls take a hit. Every guy wants to be like you, getting the hot girls. And every girl wants to be the one who catches your eye."

He shook his head. "So how do I catch the eye of the average girl?"

Ruby giggled. "Already caught my eye."

"You're not average, Rubes," they both said at once. Journey looked over at him with a spark of something in her eye.

"He's right, Ruby. You are obviously exceptional. That quiche was incredible. And look, even Blake ate it, and he's a cheddar boy."

"I am kind of amazing, aren't I?"

Journey grinned, and Cody laughed. And tipping his head back, he thought about how he could show Journey that he no longer wanted the perfect, pretend girls. He wanted average, normal, incredible Journey.

ಭಿ✤✤✤ಜ

Journey was standing in the middle of the field—the one where she could get reception—with the little flip phone pressed to her ear. It had been two weeks since the night of the dance party when she'd almost kissed Cody. Every moment since had been a practice in self-control. Tonight, her hands were shaking, and she just needed some clarity. Jenni's voice on the line took her breath away, bringing a rush of lonely tears to her eyes. "Jenni, it's me."

"I know." Jenni's voice was a whisper and then went back to her normal volume and sass. "I'm at an event right now, Hanna. Can't this wait?"

"Gosh, I've missed your voice," Journey said, her voice catching.

"I've got to take this, please excuse me," she heard Jenni say. A moment later, the background noise disappeared, and Jenni's voice came back quieter. "Oh, my word. It has been a month since you last called. I was about to send out a search party."

"I've just been busy," Journey said, swiping tears from her cheeks.

"What is it, baby girl? What's going on?"

"Nothing," Journey said. "It's all good. I just … couldn't sleep and had this horrible homesickness for Stella's curls. Why am I doing this again?"

Jenni let out a sigh. "Girl, take a deep breath. No fireflies out there?"

Journey sobbed. "None."

Jenni hummed a soothing sound. "Something's getting to you. You are solid in doing this. Helen has been on a war path, but I am so impressed in how you covered your bases. Well done."

Nodding to herself, she inhaled deeply, trying to consider the positives. "I've got a few new things in the works: I've been writing a bit and playing a lot. It feels so good to be the real me again.

Jenni laughed a little. "I cannot believe that you are doing this. Like really pulling it off. I don't know if Liz or I could be as strong as you are."

"I met this guy." Journey finally blurted.

"Yeah, I knew that was coming."

"No, Jenni. He's everything I don't need. He's just out of rehab; he's a complete pain in the butt. I can't even believe I'm telling you about him."

"Because he's also amazing?"

"Maybe, sometimes," Journey conceded, blowing her nose and then bringing the phone back to her ear.

"How does he treat you?"

"He … I haven't let him … I …"

"You're playing scared?"

"Terrified." This came out as a squeak, with more tears and a sob.

"You're telling me this, because you need to know it's okay to take it up a notch and see what happens. Girl, you are risk in a tiny package. You know how to do this. What the heck are you waiting for?"

She shook her head, taking in the darkness of the vast meadow before her, the quiet hoot of an owl swooping overhead, and the gentle hum of crickets. "I'm trying to do something I've never done before, and I'm totally afraid to screw it up."

"Look, we all screw it up. It's a part of life. Going into life scared and not making any mistakes doesn't mean you're a better person. It just means you're living half a life. Believe me when I tell you, Colin was a mistake. But that mistake gave me Stella. My life changed forever when I became a mother. Mistakes are a part of the game. I'm not saying to go crazy and mess up your life. I'm just saying, you can't do life scared, or you end up missing the most amazing parts."

Journey wiped a tear or two and nodded. "Gosh, Jen. When did you get so wise?"

Jenni giggled. "It's my motherhood gene. I swear you get a dose of wisdom with the glycogen drink when you're pregnant."

Journey laughed, putting an arm around herself. "Mistakes are okay."

"Imperative," Jenni whispered back. "That's why I'm forgiving you for not calling for a month. Don't make me worry like that again, m'kay?"

"I won't. Thank you, Jenni. Please kiss Stella for me. I love you."

Journey clicked her phone shut, sliding it into the back of her blue jeans and hugging her hoodie around her. If she thought about it like that, without the heavy pressure of perfection, it made her shoulders sink back down and stilled the sob in her throat. She sniffed, using her shirtsleeve to get the tears off her face and looked up at the sky, hoping for Grandma's blessing on what she was about to do.

With determination in her step, she turned and walked back toward the cabins.

๛✽✽✽๏

It was after dinner but too early to be in bed. Even though Cody longed to make it an early night, his brain wasn't cooperating. Despite his best efforts, it would not be still. And the more he wrote, the less he wanted to drink. When he felt the urge pressing up from inside of him, making him restless, he grabbed a pad and just started writing. He'd gone through several of the inn's versions before asking Ian to bring him up a notebook or two on his mandatory visits with his AA sponsor.

Now, he was sipping rootbeer on ice and scribbling out lyrics. Some of them were useless pieces of crap, especially when his brain was too much into the situation to let creativity happen. But when he got going, something amazing happened. It was a magic he hadn't felt since he'd signed with his current agent, successfully shoving his real dream in a broom closet.

He shook his head, scratching down a few more words. Tonight, it was a fight, a battle between thinking about all the girls he'd dated, the reasons for his interest in them, and what he was feeling for Journey. He couldn't focus for a minute on the lyrics in his head. He was too busy trying to figure out how to tell Journey he cared for more than just her body.

Her curves were amazing, but they were not the only thing that got his attention that first day. It was everything else. Her sass. Her fearlessness. Her ability to take him down in a mud puddle. Man, that made him stop and take notice.

He threw his pen down, resting his head in his hands. "How do you make a girl believe you want her for the right reasons?" he wondered aloud. He knew the person he should talk to. Any of his brothers would work, but that would mean waiting until tomorrow. Big

Ben was his best bet. The way he treated Mama Lucille was what love stories were made of.

He shoved away from the table, leaving his mess of words there. Pushing his arms into a flannel, he was out the door and crunching through the gravel. Heaven knew a brisk walk would do wonders even if he couldn't find Ben. He was headed for the inn when he saw a light in the barn and turned his course. Ben was easy to spot due to his exceptional stature. Tonight, he was putting a tool back on its peg on the wall when Cody walked in.

"Cody Blake. What's got you out tonight?"

Cody shrugged, totally unsure about how to start this conversation. "Do you ever have the problem where your brain just won't turn off?"

Ben chuckled. "Naw. That's Lucille's challenge. I sleep like a baby. Always said it had something to do with a clear conscience." Here, he winked.

Cody laughed. "Yeah, my conscience has been clearer."

"Somethin' botherin' ya?"

"I just …" He ran a hand through his hair. "I probably shouldn't be thinking about girls right now, but … what happens when you meet someone who is nothing like you ever thought you would want? And all of a sudden, your whole life—everything you planned on and worked toward—seems to be nothing but a waste of time."

Ben's grin widened. "Sounds like you're getting a dose of reality. Girls tend to make you rethink everything. Here's the thing, Cody. Us men have the habit of thinking on the short term. But when a girl like that walks into your life, you start looking through a different lens. It can be quite the shock."

"Tell me about it."

"That little red-head in there," he pointed toward the inn, "she shook up my reality the first day I met her. I had been dating quite a few ladies, all pretty much the same. I thought I knew what I liked. And then this sassy girl walks into the store. I flirted with everyone at my counter. It only seemed right. But she wanted nothing to do with me. She was unlike any of the other girls. That spark in her eye had me hooked from day one. I wanted to get her attention, that's for sure."

Cody nodded. "How'd you do it. I mean, how do you show a girl you're not messing around. Especially after being an idiot?"

Ben looked thoughtful for a minute. "Well, it's not an easy thing, is it? I've learned through forty years of marriage that trust is something that ladies rely on heavily. It starts with knowing you're going to do what you say you will, living up to a standard, ya know?

"When your real with the person you care about, you don't play games or hide behind fear. You have to be honest with your weaknesses and then commit to fight for what means the most to ya."

He took Cody by the shoulder. "Now, listen to this if you hear nothing else. A good relationship isn't one that drives along with nary a bump in the road. A relationship worth fighting for comes with detours and disappointments, along with the smooth times. The key is committing. Saying it isn't enough. You got to show up even when things get sticky. That's when it counts the most. If you're gonna do it, for heaven's sake, suck it up and stick it out. Show up when it matters most. You'll never regret it."

Ben and Cody parted ways, the darkness complete. Cody's head was down contemplating Ben's words until he was ten steps from his cabin. That's when he caught sight of her.

Chapter Eight

Out of the corner of his eye, he saw her. A double take revealed Journey Miller dressed in moonlight as she crossed the grass. He could understand now how people dreamed up mythical creatures. She looked up, her dark eyes meeting his and he stopped cold.

Was he imagining this feeling, the way his heart started racing whenever he saw her? The way she made him question everything he'd ever wanted? The way he just couldn't stop thinking about her?

There was something in her way of taking life in her little hand that made him doubt he had ever lived before.

He tried not to feel nervous as she approached. Emotions flashed through him, gratitude that he'd thought to brush his teeth, concern over the state of his hair, second thoughts on his breath. There was a smile on her lips that had his heart pounding. She never smiled at him like that.

"Where you going?" she asked when she was close enough, her hands tucked into her hoodie.

"Um … just … I just finished talking to Big Ben."

"Everything okay?" she asked, stepping so close that Cody was having a hard time keeping his train of thought.

"Yeah ... fine."

She nodded and smiled that same smile, like she knew something he didn't.

He cleared his throat. "Get any good reception out there?"

She shrugged. "Good enough." She reached out and touched one side of his flannel shirt, running her finger along the line of buttons. He thought he was going to have a heart attack.

"Journey, I need to tell you something."

She nodded. "Okay." She stepped closer so he had to clear his throat again and work on some fine control to keep from pulling her in. He never knew when she was willing to be close, and when she was on the verge of decking him.

"I know my dating history is pretty crummy," he started. Her head bobbed in understanding, looking up into his face while her left hand took the other side of his shirt and gave it a gentle tug to bring him in.

"You're in need of some remedial help in that area," she said softly.

"Yeah, I am," he agreed, giving in to the urge to slip his hands around her waist. They sank to her hips in an instant replay of the night she had cut his hair. She used her hands on his shirt fronts to pull him down, chucking the idea of personal space and lifting her lips to his.

If he was surprised, he didn't show it. He had been dreaming of this moment for weeks. He let her set the pace at first, her kiss gently teasing. Then, he pressed his hands to her back, extinguishing any distance left between them, and took over, sliding a hand up to the nape of her neck and sighing when her hands traveled up his chest and around his neck. This moment would be forever seared into his memory. Something about longing for a kiss made it that much sweeter when it actually happened.

Tonight was more than he had hoped. If her passion for country music was any indication, when she drew him close, she had every intention of showing him how she felt. The sensation of her fingertips in his hair, the hum of her breath, and the way she returned his kisses had his head spinning.

She pulled back for a moment, and he groaned. "Please don't stop."

"I'm not going to," she laughed.

"Good, because I have been hoping to do this for a while now."

She slid a finger along his jaw line. "Cody, I'm really afraid you're going to crush my heart into a thousand tiny pieces."

He sighed. "I don't have the best track record, Journey. But I swear, being here has changed me. Being around you has made me a different person ... or at least, maybe it's made me remember the kind of guy I wanted to be."

"I want you to be that kind of guy too," she said softly, driving him insane by tracing the line of his lower lip with her fingertip.

"Does this mean you don't hate me anymore?" he asked, breathlessly.

Journey's smirk was one of the sexiest things he'd ever seen. "You tell me," she whispered, bringing her mouth to his again, her fingers gently weaving through his hair while her heartbeat told him that she had indeed changed her mind.

※※※※※

When Cody and Journey walked into the inn holding hands thirty minutes later, and edged up to the counter looking for Ruby, they found Mama Lucille and Big Ben instead. Journey released Cody's hand the minute she remembered he wasn't supposed to be dating while doing his community service. Dang. This could be bad.

"Good evening, Mr. Blake. Journey. How was your day?" Lucille had a look on her face that said she knew what going on, even if they weren't going to own up to it.

"It was great." Journey said, trying to be chill about her response.

Give up nothing.

Unreadable face.

Calm breathing.

Do my lips look like we've just been making out for a half-hour?

Is it possible to look like you've just been kissed?

The very thought made her want to draw him close right then and there and see if it could be done. He was a great kisser.

Cody smiled at her, the smile that made all the girls swoon and made her heart race now that she wasn't pretending she didn't like him. He turned to Ben and Lucille. "I'm glad you're here. Can we have a moment?"

Journey gaped at Cody for split second before recovering herself. What was he doing? If they told Lucille and Ben, they wouldn't be able to see each other until after his hours of community service were done at the inn. Yesterday, that would have settled just fine with her, but right this minute, when she was daydreaming of the next time they would kiss and hoping it would be very soon, that would not work out at all.

Lucille nudged Ben's shoulder. He had been eating a sandwich at the counter when they walked in and hadn't seemed to notice what was taking place.

He looked up. "Hey there, kids." A look from Lucille, and he was standing, dusting off his hands, and looking longingly at the sandwich.

"Won't be a minute, honey," Lucille chuckled. "We'll make sure no garden gnomes abscond with your sandwich."

"Not the gnomes I worry about," Ben said with a smile, following after Cody and Journey who trailed Lucille.

In the small office, made tighter by Ben's stature, Journey looked around hesitantly. Cody wasted no time, his voice steady, his face earnest.

"I came here under some pretty rough circumstances. I wasn't happy, and I'm sure you could tell. But that was six weeks ago, and to be honest, I can't even remember what that person was like. If rehab started the change in me, no matter how reluctant, being here has sent it a long way down the path I hope to stay on. I can't thank you enough for giving me this opportunity."

Lucille was all quiet listening, her face soft and open. Ben was leaning forward, one hip resting on the desk, and Journey could see some understanding dawning on him. The grin working itself outside his control was wide.

"That being said, I know one of the rules was that I couldn't date while I was here. I'm ... asking for some leniency in that area. Not so that I can pursue your guests," he quickly added, shooting a glance at Ben and then a quick look at Journey.

"Then why would you be wantin' us to do that, Cody," Ben said in his thoughtful way. Journey turned to Cody and watched. She had *not* expected this. She was expecting to sneak behind the cabins at night or kiss in the forest when they weren't busy. She felt her heart start to race in anticipation of what was to come.

"Journey is someone I want to get to know better. We could do it behind your backs like a couple of high schoolers, but I'd rather not risk my community service or offend you two. More than that ... I've done things backwards and upside-down for a while now when it comes to the ladies I've dated. My momma taught me better. With Journey ..." He looked at her for a long moment, and Journey felt something swell inside her chest. There was something in his face that said more than, "I think you have a smokin' hot body." It thrilled and scared her all at once. "With Journey, I want to *be* better. She deserves it. And thank the Lord she knows it."

Lucille chuckled, and Journey was sure she saw a glint of something in her eyes before she swiped it away.

"What do you think, Ben?"

"Well, the stipulations of no fraternizing came from Mama and I. I'd say we can wave them as good as we can enforce them. But sayin' that, on the job is no time to be making moves on your lady. Keep it PG and take care of our guests just the same as you did before and we'll be happy with ya." Ben shook a finger during his moment of warning and then returned to his wide grin.

Cody's grin matched his. "You got it. Thank you, both."

"Yep," Ben returned. Lucille just smiled, nodding her head at the two of them as they walked out, this time not hiding the hands they were holding. Outside the office door, Cody pulled her aside, slid his hands around her waist, and kissed her firmly.

"That was scary."

"Almost like facing a dad with a well-polished shotgun, huh?" Journey giggled.

"Worse. Ben could break me in two with those huge hands," Cody said, looking down into her face with a laugh.

"Now we have to face something scarier." Journey leaned in, gently rubbing her nose against Cody's.

His eyes widened, and his head reared back. "What?"

"Ruby."

ಸಿ❋❋❋ಲ

Ruby was finishing up a late-night snack for the guests when they found her. "I miss everything," she moaned, tossing a towel over her shoulder and landing it on the burner of the stove. It quickly caught on fire, and Dante stepped over and placed a metal lid over it, extinguishing the burner with a flick of his wrist. He shot Journey a long suffering look, and she tried not to smile. Oh, boy, did he know he was on accident prevention as well as general sous-chef duties when he was hired at Snowflake Falls kitchen?

"It *just* happened," Journey soothed, trying not to be distracted by the fact that she was perched on Cody's knee instead of a seat of her own.

"Just …" Ruby blew out a breath and shook her tongs at the two of them in between turning scones frying in hot oil in front of her. "I saw it coming weeks ago, people. The minute I knew *she* didn't like *you,* it was kind of obvious Fate would do this twisty thing. Almost inevitable."

She tossed some of the cooked scones into a cinnamon, sugar, and nutmeg mixture and then popped them onto two plates. "I should be jealous, because I think he was into me first," Ruby said, her brows lifted, not meeting their eyes. But then she turned her grin on them. "But you're so darn cute, and I've been dying to see if I would win the bet!"

"Bet?" Journey and Cody looked at each other.

"Yeah. Grady, the produce guy at the farmer's market—he saw you two when you went for eggs?"

"I remember him. Young guy. Kind of short. Wears a baseball cap?" Cody asked.

"*Always* wears a baseball cap. Yeah. He's the one. He saw you two, and when we talked the next week when I went up for those darling baby asparagus—remember?—he bet me that you would kiss in two weeks, and I bet him one, and here we are. You with your kissing, and me with a whole crate of fresh peaches next time I see him. O'Henry. My favorite for peach tarts."

"You bet a whole crate of peaches on us kissing?" Journey wanted to be offended, but she was too interested in these peach tarts and how soon she could sample one.

"Well, don't get huffy. I was going to have to cook *him* a dinner. I think we both know who would have gotten the better end of that deal."

"For sure," Journey agreed.

"He thinks you're hot," Cody interjected.

Both girls stopped and looked at him. His hand on Journey's waist tightened just a smidge.

"What? What did you say?" Ruby asked, her forehead scrunched up under the bright can lights of the kitchen.

"He thinks you're hot. No guy bets a girl dinner without thinking she's hot. Money, okay. That's a hand-off. He wanted to spend an evening with you, Ruby."

"Ooo! Ruby's got an admirer."

Ruby shook her head. "No way. Grady is ..." She tried to use her hands to explain, wringing them this way and then the other way, as she searched the ceiling for words to express it right. "The hat thing. He wears *overalls*."

"Who saved you the best baby asparagus?" Journey asked.

Ruby's eyes went big. "Oh. My. Word. Come to think of it, he also made sure I got the cabbages I wanted. Purple, not green, and about 8.5 inches across because bigger gives me a headache to chop and smaller is just a waste of time ..." Her voice trailed off, and she forgot she was turning scones, so her assistant rushed over again, grasping the tongs and filling in.

Journey and Cody looked at each other and grinned. Ruby was the best.

~ ❖ ❖ ❖ ~

The next morning, Cody was waiting on her porch when Journey walked out the door. He had a cup of cocoa in each hand and a kiss waiting for her. Her hands slid around his waist, leaning into the kiss, and enjoying the softness of his lips and the gentle tickle of his neatly trimmed beard. Oh, boy.

"Thought you might like some cocoa, with whipped cream," he said, his breath warm against her lips.

She grinned, pressing another kiss to his mouth. "Hand whipped by Ruby? I could get used to this."

"Believe me, I was thinking the same thing," he growled, kissing her more fervently.

Before they could become a spectacle, Journey stepped back, accepting her cup and leading the way to the inn. "What do we have this morning?" she asked.

"Five sisters. You won't believe this, but they all have a name that starts with B."

Journey cut a look over her shoulder to be sure he wasn't teasing. "All of them?"

"Yeah. Ben briefed me this morning when I went in to get the cocoa. Annual sisters retreat. His words were, 'They're something else,' which probably means they're all loony."

Journey slowed enough to slip her arm through Cody's. Okay, she enjoyed leaning against his well-muscled frame more than she wanted to admit. She was still wondering how this happened, but it was one more thing she could work into her schedule.

"Or it could mean they're lots of fun. You thought I was loony at first."

He stopped so he could wrap an arm around her back and sneak one more kiss. "No, I thought you were a pain in the butt, and I was totally right."

She accepted his kiss and then walked into the inn, stopping by the kitchen for a breakfast sandwich—that Ruby delivered with a wink—before meeting the group in the lobby.

There are all kinds of sisters. Some don't get along, some are bosom buddies, and others merely tolerate one another. The room that Journey entered while nibbling a bit of sausage from her sandwich was filled to bursting, not because there were five women there, dressed in various stages of hiking gear, but because of their energy.

Excitement bounced off the walls with the laughter and chatter. One woman, with hair that stood up on her head in a fancy, short style, was talking to Cody. He noticed Journey walk in and raised his brows. She couldn't tell whether he was happy to see her or begging her to call for the cavalry.

"Are these the five B ladies?"

"That's us," the woman beside Cody said. "I'm Betsie." She pointed to each of the ladies in the room in turn. "This is Belinda, Benevolence, Britta, and Beth."

"Mom thought naming us all B names was clever," Britta sniggered.

"I think Dad was just trying to use our initial as an excuse to not remember our names."

"It worked," Beth laughed. "We all looked up at once."

"You don't have to call me Belinda. Bel is just fine," the one in the floppy hat said.

"And I'm Bennie," Benevolence said. Journey made a note of all their names and motioned them outside.

"Well, the weather today is lovely. Why don't we get started while you tell us more about yourselves and why you're here at the inn?"

Cody took up the rear, talking with the shortest one—Betsie, Journey thought. With a little outward puff of breath, she considered their dad a genius and thought she may resort to calling out, 'B,' and letting every head swivel her way.

"We've all got a gift," said Bel, who fell into step beside her. "It helps to keep us sorted."

"Is that right?" Journey turned to her with interest. Bel had short gray hair treated with the typical grandma curls hidden under her hat. Her figure was gently rounded, but her blue eyes were sharp and intelligent.

"Yes. I suppose we grew up with a hippie twist to things. I'd say we just had the leg up on getting to know our life's purpose, where most people don't get that figured out for a while."

"Life's purpose? You have this figured out?"

"Mm hmm." Bel hummed as they climbed a bit of a hill and then leveled out to continue up toward the summit of a nearby mountain. This wasn't a high-level hike, but it was one where there were moments of concentration and effort that would steal their breath.

Journey took the time to contemplate her words. Life's purpose. She thought she knew something about her life's purpose. Music was obviously a part of what she wanted to do with her life. Family would come later, and a good relationship with it. She toyed with the idea of these things being her life's purpose, the reason she was born on the earth and came up feeling a little less than sure of herself.

"Chewed on that long enough?" Bel shot her a look, and Journey turned to her in surprise.

"I suppose I'm curious about your gifts."

"Well that's a good place to start." Bel grinned. Her teeth were white and even, except for one on the bottom that jostled it's way tightly amongst the others. The imperfection only added to the charm of her smile.

"Let's see now, I'm a healer. I just have the knack for setting bones and birthing babies. I do more birthing babies than messing with broken bones these days."

"That sounds like a pretty rewarding profession," Journey said.

"One of the best ways to live your life is helping other people bring life into the world. I don't think I've ever had a bad day on the job." Bel agreed.

"You've never lost a baby? That's incredible."

Bel shook her head, puffing for another minute. "Didn't say that. But then, I'm not conventional in my thinking about life and death. Death doesn't have to be a horrible thing."

Journey's brows drew together. "It has been in my experience." Bel searched her face for a long moment and then went on.

"Betsie's good at sensing when there's trouble. That's what makes her an incredible nurse. Bennie's an empath. She can literally sense the moods in the air. She went into marriage and family therapy. Britta's main gift is being a smarty pants. She has an IV drip of sarcasm hooked up every single morning, and she's still used it all up by midday. While she's busy being a pain in the butt, she's also noticing a lot of things people overlook. She's a crime scene investigator, so you can imagine those skills come in real handy."

Journey turned to look at the group of ladies behind her. One of them, Britta, she assumed, because she had a baseball cap on that had a police department logo, was saying something while the rest of them, including Cody, laughed.

"And then there's Beth. From the minute you meet her, you'll love her. She's the charmer. Being a lawyer is natural for her, because she tends to get whatever she wants. It helps a lot when you're trying to coordinate a flight for five sisters from all over the nation. People just naturally want to help her," Bel giggled.

"You have an incredible family," Journey said, feeling a pang of something like jealousy. If she were to designate obvious gifts to her sisters, Liz would get the snark-on-command gene and mad skills with clothing design. Jen knew how to work a makeup brush like no other. Neither of them were doing anything life altering with their skills, nothing in the line of a life's purpose. "And I can see how each of their vocations make the world a better place."

"Oh, it's not about the work we do, though I think our gifts have definitely influenced that." Bel shrugged. "It's more what we do with our free time."

"What do you do with your free time?"

Bel grinned. "Well, since you asked, I served a mission at the beginning of this summer, helping in Greece with the incredible influx of refugees, all of them needing medical care and in some state of emotional trauma. Took the sisters with me. You can't imagine how helpful they all were.

"Beth's gift may seem kind of self-serving, but the truth is, with her help, people were literally emptying their pockets, bending over backwards to get us desperately needed supplies, generally willing to do more than they might otherwise have done. She's got the Jedi mind tricks down pat."

Journey grinned. "Wow, sounds like quite a trip."

"If you could see what we've seen. Entire families frozen to the bone from enduring a boat trip with only the barest necessities in their possession. Many have lost their livelihoods, their homes, their professions, and their standing in their communities, and all are brought to the same level of needing relief. It's pretty humbling."

"It must be nice to come to the inn and have a real vacation after that," Journey said, not sure what she was feeling inside, this desire to figure out her own life's purpose. It sounded terrifying, yet like the most important thing she could ever discover.

"We're actually here to regroup. Like I said, we live all around the country and it's nice to be together and talk about what to do next. There's still a great deal of need in Greece, but there's also a lot to be done wherever these refugee families are being placed. Many are finding homes here in the states as well, you know?"

"I heard," Journey said, studying her companion from the side. The woman looked undisturbed about the whole idea, not fearful at all. "A lot of people are afraid of them, you know? Worried about terror attacks and the like."

Bel nodded. "Sure. We're all worried about that. Most of those who come from those camps want nothing more than to find a way to live again, a way to make their lives up from the ground where they've crumbled. Sure, there will be those, just like here among our countrymen, who do terrible deeds. I don't doubt it. But there are so many who just need a way to start over."

The sun spilled out onto the trail up ahead as though it were pointing out a divine moment in time. Journey looked up at the white puffs of clouds and followed the trails of sunbeams shooting down from the heavens. What would happen when they reached that patch of glorious brightness, she wondered.

"How did you find out what your life's purpose was?" Journey asked. It was a question gnawing at her since the phrase first came up in their conversation. Does one just *know* what they are meant to do? Do they discover it after long searching? Was it a calling like religious people often felt?

"It's pretty simple, in my opinion," Bel said, swiping some sweat from her brow and replacing her hat.

"First of all, you have to believe your life is meant for greatness."

Journey's brows rose. "Greatness?"

"Yeah, you know, for more than simple monotony, solely to be entertained or to work endlessly with no overarching purpose."

Journey thought about Grandma. She knew that Grandma June believed there was more to life than simple execution of bucket list items and then death. She believed doing good, even a little everyday was what was most important. Journey felt goose bumps down her arms. Ooo … she was onto something.

"My grandma thought something like that too."

"Your grandma sounds like a wise woman," Bel said with a wide smile. "Once you know you're on the earth for more than a pleasurable life focused on feeding your selfish desires, you start to look around and see what needs doing, what calls to you."

Journey thought about this for a moment while they climbed the last bit to the summit of the mountain.

"Is that how you found your purpose?"

"It's how I *find* my purpose. It changes, you know? At first, it was getting enough education to do something positive in the world. To be a force for good. Birthing babies has been an enlightening experience. At first, I thought that was enough. But then, I came to a point of restlessness. My kids were grown, doing good things of their own, and I realized my purpose needed reevaluation. It's something I do consistently, taking a look every time I start to lose my sense of peace."

Bel looked down at the green expanse of hills, tree tops, and meadows before them. The lake yawned its way in the midst, a bright, sparkling blue. The bridge provided a geometric line to the scene. Fresh pine and earth filled the air with every breath.

"There's rain coming," Betsie said from the other side of the group. They all looked up and noticed what Journey had missed during her intense conversation to the summit. The fluffy white clouds had been shoved to the side by a crowded gray mass that indeed looked intent on rain.

"Dang, Cody, those look serious."

"Yeah, we'd better get you ladies down pretty quickly. Weather patterns change like lightning up here."

Journey watched Cody take the arms of Bennie and Betsie. The trail was steep at this portion, and he worked to make sure no one lost their footing. Britta and Beth were in the middle, and Bel took up the rear with Journey. They were hurrying, quickly side stepping over rocks. There was cursing and laughing when the clouds looming above gutted themselves over their heads.

"Told you we should have brought umbrellas," Betsie crowed. "Think they'll listen to me now?" This question was directed at Cody who had her arm.

"I will," Cody said.

"Ah, nothing like hiking in the rain," Beth laughed, doing a little dance on the trail. She nearly twisted her ankle, and Journey lunged just in time to catch her arm and steady her. The rain was nothing like the gentle storms that they had hiked in before. This one was big fat drops dumped out by the bucketful. The dirt trail was quickly morphing into a riverbed.

"Adventure awaits!" Bennie called back over her shoulder.

Journey wiped the rain out of her eyes, pointing to a rocky overhang nearby.

"Let's wait it out, Cody." She had to yell it over the pounding rain and laughing ladies around her.

They veered, tromping through mud puddles and sloshing through ponds to the shelter of rocks. It did much to block out the downpour.

Journey looked over at Bel, and they both started laughing. Oh, boy, did they look a sight! Every head was drenched, hair lying flat and plastered to their heads, shirts soaked through, and eyelashes dripping. Even with their hats, Bel and Britta were drenched.

Journey looked to Cody next and found him staring at her. Oh, my. The look in his eyes stirred something warm in her belly. She wished they were all alone against the rocks, soaking wet and doing more than looking at one another with an audience.

"Well, then." Bennie grinned.

Journey tore her eyes from Cody's face, indulging a lingering glance at his well-muscled chest. The way his tee clung to his skin didn't help matters. Instead she turned her attention to the scene before her. The trail was quickly deteriorating and they still had a mile to go to get back to the inn.

Cody was in front of her a moment later, his hand taking hers quietly. Dark heat spread up through her arm when she looked up at him, but he was all business despite repeatedly getting distracted by her lips.

"I think we should make a break for it. We're as wet as we can get. It might end up getting worse if we wait. The other option would be for me to make a run for the Ranger."

Journey nodded, looking up into his face. Gosh, he looked amazing with water droplets in his hair. "We can probably make it down together, but let's see if they're up for it."

"Done with your powwow, or is this going to break into a make out session?" Britta asked. Ah, there was the promised sarcasm.

"We have a choice to make ladies," Cody said. "Make a go of it, or wait here while I run for the Ranger to carry you out in style."

"We came for a hike, I'd say," Bennie said after a moment of thought. "Why not finish it out? Nothing more than the refugees go through on a daily basis."

"Remember when it rained for three days straight in Greece? Every tent was floating." Beth put in.

"That one family had a new baby the next night. I almost suggested Noah for a name." Bel laughed.

"Well, let's go then, shall we?" Britta took the lead, peeking out at the sheets of water falling in front of them and then motioning for all to follow her.

There was some slipping. A few close calls. It was when Bel slipped that Journey found herself face down in mud. At first, she was only trying to keep Bel on her feet. None of them needed a broken hip on their conscience. But when she reached out to steady her companion, she didn't notice the rock protruding from the ground, dug out by rainwater rushing down the trail.

Five minutes more, and it would have been entirely unearthed and rushing on it's merry way. But Journey hit it with the tip of her shoe when she wasn't looking and that made her come down on her ankle in the worst possible position. Her joint gave way, and she just missed kissing the trail the next instant, her ankle throbbing in a way that can't just be walked off.

"Woman down!" Bel bellowed into the rain.

Chapter Nine

She had to bellow because the pounding of those fierce droplets was its own drum section, all bass fury with no melody line to give it body.

Cody was beside her in a moment. They looked at each other, wetter than ever. "How bad?"

Journey felt a twinge of comfort that he didn't think she was a wimp. "I don't think I can walk on it."

Bel was kneeling down beside her, her khaki trousers soaking in dark mud as she gently probed the joint.

"Ah ... it's not broken, but you shouldn't give the mountain another try. I'd say elevation and ice is the ticket."

Journey looked back at Cody with a bit of bleakness in her face. Elevation wasn't a possibility at the moment.

"I'll carry you," he offered. "Trust me?"

It felt like he was asking about more than just confidence in being toted down a slippery-slide mountain trail. For an instant, she wondered if she was ready to put herself in his hands. Kissing was amazing. Holding him was one of her favorite new things to do. But was she ready to hand over her heart?

Instead of thinking too hard, she nodded. "Okay."

"Piggy back?"

Another nod, and he turned while Bel helped her to her knees. Cody used his thighs to propel them from the sodden earth.

"They'll do anything to cuddle," Bennie shouted, a teasing chuckle carrying through the rain.

"You know it," Journey said, gritting her teeth against the pain in her ankle. While the first half of the journey had been enlightening in one way, the second half taught her a couple of things about the man she was learning to trust.

First, he was strong and capable, but not just in a fashion magazine kind of way. The muscles he had weren't just for looks. The trail became more hazardous with every passing minute. He wasn't just toting her, he was also watching out for the five sisters. He led the way, calling out warnings to the women behind him, doing his best to choose the safest route.

Second, he didn't give up when things got messy. They were nearly to the base of the steepest section when his footing gave way. It happened incredibly fast, and everyone felt helpless to give him aid. Journey felt herself falling and let go, sliding down onto her good leg that just kept on going, bringing her first to her bum and then to her back before she could stop the momentum. If they'd been a muddy mess that first day, they were no less so at this moment. When she looked up she was surrounded by sisters and the face of a guy who had totally dropped her.

"Journey, I'm so sorry. I lost my footing—" His voice was rough, near tears.

"Stop. I'm okay. This is a terrible situation, so let's just not get crazy about it."

He shook his head. "I'm sorry."

She didn't care if the sisters were watching and they had promised Lucille and Ben to keep the PDA under control. She pushed herself up, gently grabbed his face with muddy hands, and pressed her lips to his for a long, fervent kiss. Even with her ankle throbbing, the rain thundering down over them, and a pretty good audience, that kiss was amazing.

"Let's get out of here," she whispered against his lips.

He nodded. "Sounds good to me. Ready?"

She nodded, and the group around them cheered.

"This is better than a movie," Betsie said as they helped Journey onto Cody's back again.

Taking even greater care, Cody worked them down to the meadow, and from there, past the cabins. Journey had never seen a happier sight than that welcoming back porch of Snowflake Falls Inn. She hunkered down, pressing her cheek to Cody's muddy shoulder and feeling grateful. Grateful that she had trusted this guy to carry her out of danger. Grateful she hadn't lost faith when he dropped her. And grateful that the end was even better than the beginning.

❦❦❦

Ruby was bouncing up onto the balls of her feet when Cody stumbled up to the porch. "They're here, they're here!" she called into the inn. Lucille, hood pulled up to shield her hair and walkie talkie in hand, appeared with Ben right behind her. His shoulders were draped in an enormous poncho.

"Thank goodness," Lucille breathed.

"Those clouds came out of nowhere," Ben grumbled, casting a narrowed glance at the sky.

"What an adventure!" Bennie crowed, her hair plastered to her head, her smile beaming.

"What's this all about," Ruby asked. She pointed to the whole muddy mess of the couple before her. Journey worked to slowly slide down Cody's back to the porch without putting pressure on her throbbing ankle.

"I fell," Journey admitted, though she'd been working on another more dramatic tale earlier.

"Don't try to pretend," Bel grinned over her shoulder, "She was really trying to get out of hiking down that hill."

"She could have chosen a better mode of transport," Cody was leaning against one of the beams that supported the back porch, his breathing still heavy, "I proved less than faithful."

"You were wonderful," Journey countered.

"So, you're hurt then," Lucille cut to the chase.

"Almost all my pride and then a little of my ankle," Journey said, trying to put a smile with her words. Despite the ache in her leg, she really was more mess than injury. Cody stepped back to her side when he noticed her wince.

Ruby held up a scolding finger and then looked as though she were rethinking her approach. She settled with folding her arms across her chef's coat. "We were getting kind of worried here. But I suppose it's nothing a good hot cup of cocoa and a bit of pie won't help."

"Now you're talking," Britta chimed in. That set off a whole round of appreciative agreement. Mmm ... hot cocoa did sound good now that her teeth were chattering.

Lucille grabbed Journey's free hand and squeezed it gently. "Now, let's get you cleaned up and take care of that ankle."

"I can do that," announced Bel. She'd removed her hat and fluffed the dry hair beneath it. Though her legs were muddy from the knee down, she still wore that bright smile. "Just wash off all that mud, get as comfy as you can, and let me know when you're ready."

"I'll take her to her cabin to get cleaned up." Cody still had his arm around Journey's waist, the warmth of his hand radiating into her midsection.

"I better come along," Lucille said, tapping Ben's arm. He produced an umbrella on cue. She grinned up at him and stood on tiptoe to kiss his cheek.

The group quickly dissipated, the sisters hurrying into the inn to wash up and get warm after their adventure. The trio worked their way to the cabin. When Lucille offered the sheltering protection of her umbrella, Cody and Journey insisted that any rain at this point would only help their situation. As it was, they left muddy prints on the porch before stepping into the cabin.

"How … long should I give you?" Suddenly, Cody looked flushed.

"I'll stay in case she needs something," Lucille said. "I'll come after you when she's had time to clean up and feel human again."

"Besides, you could use a bit of the same treatment, cowboy." Journey tossed this over her shoulder as Lucille took her arm and helped her limp to the bathroom.

Cody didn't move for a lingering moment before blowing out a long breath and turning toward his cabin to get washed up.

ಜಿ❄❄❄ಲ

While Journey had been scrubbing black dirt from every conceivable nook and cranny, Ruby had been in the kitchen baking up a storm. Bel met Journey on a couch in the gathering room. Following a quick once-over, a bandage was expertly wrapped, giving her ankle much needed support.

Bel had such a gentle touch to go with her excellent sense of humor. "If that hike down the mountain doesn't seal the deal, I don't know what will," she whispered, and then giggled as she leaned back to finish wrapping Journey's sprain. "I think if I ever had a man's biceps wrapped around my thighs like that, I'd say yes the minute he asked me."

Journey turned three shades of red. "We're just dating."

"Just …" Bel laughed, resting hands on her thighs from where she sat on a low stool. "Well, just be kind enough to send your wedding invites to the five B girls, won't you? We'd love to see how this one turns out."

Journey couldn't stop blushing. She thought her hair would be red by the time Bel stopped. But Bel seemed to sense that she was making her uncomfortable, even if she wasn't Bennie.

"Now, two days off this foot and you should be good to go. Take it from a mom of four, you won't get many days like these, so let them wait on you a bit, 'kay?"

Journey agreed to this with a willing heart. She hadn't quite outgrown her enjoyment of being waited on as Isabelle Atkins. Nothing sounded better than lying back, catching up on some reading, and maybe kissing Cody.

Once cocooned in her blanket with her foot at the proper elevation and a cold compress taking down the swelling, Ruby wheeled out a little cart simply overflowing with deliciousness.

Journey groaned, knowing her willpower had slipped down the drain with the suds and mud from her shower. Her stomach growled like a mountain lion, and she was more than ready to appease it by throwing it a few delicacies, a hearty bowl of something steaming, and a homemade roll complete with yummy glaze.

"Oh, Rubes. You know the way to a girl's heart," Journey said as Ruby set up a little wooden side table for her meal.

"Hey, I thought food was the way to a *guy's* heart," Cody said, walking into the room and looking way too good with a fresh pair of jeans, a button up that hugged his muscular shoulders and biceps, and hair that was still wet from the shower.

"I guess in this case it works both ways. I'll have you both in love with me by nightfall." Ruby giggled. "Now, for you." She whipped her head around to Journey, her blue eyes thoughtful. "I made two soups just in case you weren't feeling creamy, but you usually like creamy."

"Cream is my life." Journey nodded willingly.

"Oh, good. This is Creamy Chicken and Wild Rice." Ruby sighed happily. "To die for, because I only use organic, washed wild rice, so there's that, plus the cream." She giggled to herself again while using a silver ladle to scoop soup into an oversized mug the color of gingerbread.

Journey gratefully accepted it into her hands, letting the delicious warmth seep in between her fingertips and down her arms. She took a tentative sip and, oh my, it was even better than she'd hoped.

"I added the orange glaze to these rolls just for you. And you always like lemon pie." Ruby was loading up a plate with every item she indicated. Orange rolls, lemon pie, oreo truffles dusted in powdered sugar, and finally, deconstructed caramel apples, complete with rich brown caramel, chocolate shavings, and sprinkles of broken pecans over slices of granny smith apple.

Journey just watched her, mesmerized, and wondered what kinds of dreams she would have with all this sugar in her system. "I could take just one bite of everything," she reasoned to herself, though there was a part of her which doubted very deeply that she had that level of self-restraint.

"Ruby, you're a saint."

"I know." Ruby's smile slipped for a moment. "Just so you know, I was totally faking complete composure out there. That storm coming up all sudden-like, and then you and Cody hobbling up like you'd just crawled out of the swamp? That totally freaked me out, Journey Miller. Don't do that again."

"It's just a sprain, Ruby. It happens all the time when you hike around the mountains in the rain."

"Believe me," Cody said, "Journey was the last person I thought would go down today. I was afraid it would be one of the B ladies. Honestly, I'd much rather give you a piggy-back than anyone else."

"They all thought you were adorable," Journey teased. "You know you were flirting with Beth."

"Beth was really sweet, for a grandma." Cody grinned, reaching over and trying to steal one of her apple slices before being batted away by Ruby. "But there's no one quite like you, Journey."

"Aww," Ruby sighed. "Okay, I'll make you a plate too."

Cody made a sign of success. "Yes!"

A platter filled with goodness of every kind, another steaming mug or two of soup, and all three settled in to enjoy themselves. Ruby had put the kitchen on autopilot for the night with her second-in-command taking over and keeping all orders running smoothly. Journey loved the time with her friends and liked it even better when Cody helped to move her so he was holding her in his lap, her back propped against a pillow. Her head was able to rest on his chest, her ankle still happily propped up under pillows.

That was how they spent the evening until everyone was yawning and stuffed far too much to even contemplate eating again for the next week.

Without much conversation, Ruby kissed Journey's head and went off to bed. Cody helped Journey to her feet—well, her foot—and they hobbled to her cabin where she insisted he should leave her on the porch. She was much too tempted to invite him in and knew it would be hard not to ask him to stay.

"Thanks for all that you did on the mountain." Journey's eyes were exactly level with his third button down.

"My pleasure," he whispered.

She tipped her head up and accepted the kiss she had been hoping for all night.

Chapter Ten

Maybe it was the sugar rush from the cookie truffles, or maybe it was just the culmination of a particularly crazy day, but her head was full. Full of thoughts about her life's purpose. Full of Cody and how much she was coming to like him.

Maybe even love him.

When she thought about it like that, there was a little gnawing in her overstuffed stomach. A feeling like maybe it wasn't completely cool to be kissing a guy who didn't even know her real name, or at the least, whom she had been before Snowflake Falls. It made her put her hands on his chest and gently separate them sooner than she would have liked. He looked down in all his tall, dark, handsome glory and ran a strong finger gently along her jawline.

"Today was pretty crazy, Journey girl. I can't tell you how glad I am that I get to kiss you at the end of it all."

Journey smiled, looking up shyly into his eyes, now cast into shadow by the overhang of the cabin porch. "I like kissing you too."

"But I should probably let you rest and get that ankle up," he finally sighed. "Sure you don't need help getting settled?"

Journey turned toward her door, leaning on the casing as she answered, "You would *not* settle me down."

He chuckled, and she felt him close behind her, the warmth of his body and the heat from his breath filling up the chilly space between them that pushed its way in when they parted. She was so tempted to spend a few more minutes out there on the porch, but her head had started to throb a little, and she still had a lot to figure out before sleep would find her tonight.

"Good night, Cody," she said, her voice a breath of whisper at the door.

"G'night, Journey." He grinned at her and then walked away, easing into the darkness outside her porch lights. His footsteps crunched in the gravel of the pathway, his shadow gently joining with the others until she closed the door and found her way to bed.

ಜ❊❊❊ಲ

"Have you ever thought about your life's purpose?" Journey was up on the bridge. The Ranger had been her chariot tonight. Her ankle was miles better after two days of resting. Well, kind of resting. The whole laying on the couch idea had been nixed by ten o'clock the first day. While her body was willing, Journey's mind was incapable of sitting still for two days. She'd found a way to gather her music and scour through it while still keeping her ankle propped up. She wrote and fine-tuned with a focus she hadn't had in weeks.

Despite that focus, Bel's words from the hike hadn't left her mind. She was finally feeling good enough to take it to Grandma on the bridge.

"I think maybe you did," Journey continued, her one-sided conversation filling up the mountain air with each puffy exhale. "Because every memory has you helping someone or heading up some committee."

She ran a hand through her hair, wishing, just this once, Grandma would really appear to talk to her and help her figure out what she needed to know. As much as she'd been thinking, her heart was unsettled. Bel said it would be something that spoke to her, but to be honest, nothing felt right.

"I thought I would find you up here." Lucille appeared at the end of the bridge, her shoes barely making a sound on the wooden planks as she approached Journey. Journey sat in the darkness of the night, wrapped in a sweatshirt that smelled deliciously of Cody Blake. Lucille had her own flannel jacket zipped up, her hands tucked into the pockets at her waist. "Doing all right, Journey girl?"

"Just ... thinking." Journey paused, feeling that familiar rush of goose bumps and knowing Grandma was near. A funny thought struck her as she looked up at Lucille, the moon creating a halo around her red curls. Just maybe, Grandma had sent her someone with her same Grandma heart to hash out the details of her soul and her purpose. She sent a grateful smile to the dark sky above her.

"Care if I sit?"

"Please." Journey patted a place beside her and Lucille sank down.

"The trouble is getting myself back up," Lucille admitted.

"I'll help you," Journey said, a smile brightening her face. It took her a moment to reign in the emotion that filled her heart when she considered that her grandma was still watching over her in such a personal way.

"You've been busy these last few days, Journey."

Journey nodded. "I haven't had this kind of uninterrupted time in a while. I think I've got some good stuff."

"I heard you playing something this morning. It was real catchy."

Journey felt a rush of color touch her cheeks. "Thank you."

"I hope you're still considering that karaoke night?"

"Yeah, this Friday actually."

"Oh, good." Lucille put both hands on her knees, her legs crossed beneath her.

Journey took a deep breath and then jumped in to keep herself from chickening out. "Can I ask you something?"

Lucille tipped her head in a gesture of acceptance. She must have known something was on Journey's mind.

"Have you ever … had a life purpose?" Once the words were out they felt lame. Like she was asking Lucille if she wanted spiritual direction from the Dalai Lama. Lucille's face didn't reflect any such feelings. There was a soft silence as she contemplated her answer, and Journey let it lay there, stretching itself catlike after a long nap.

"Why do you ask?" she said finally, shifting her position so she could look at Journey better.

Journey chewed on a corner of her mouth. "The other day—the one where everything went crazy? When we were hiking, one of the B sisters talked about having a life purpose, and how it can change and how most of the time it means doing something good for the world. Even with everything that happened afterward, I can't get that thought out of my mind."

Lucille's smile was a slow, steadily growing one as Journey spoke.

"Well, I am certainly happy to hear it, Journey. I cannot imagine you any other way. It takes some people a lot longer to discover their life's purpose or even to contemplate one at all. There are those who enjoy a more hedonistic approach to life in general and don't find themselves too concerned about anything besides their own selfish pursuits. I'm afraid much of the younger generation has attached themselves to this kind of mindset."

Journey could only nod. Oh, my, had they. A vision of her sisters, and her mother especially, socked her right in the stomach. Life purpose to them was the pursuit of luxury of every kind. She had been caught up in it for far too long.

"I know what you mean."

"You know, it only takes one person living their life authentically to start a movement," Lucille said, turning her blue eyes toward Journey. Journey took in her open and lovely face. There was something genuine about the laugh lines around her eyes and the way her skin had softly begun to wrinkle in all the normal places. It was something her mother would find horrific in so many ways, and yet tonight under the moon, it was the most beautiful thing she had ever seen.

"I'm not sure how to go about it," Journey said finally. "I feel this ... desire ... to do something, to find my life's purpose. But how in the world does one do it?"

"For me," Lucille said, pulling one knee up toward her chest and looking up toward the full light of the moon, "it began with something that struck up a passion inside of me. Something that felt like home." She looked at me with a frown. "That probably doesn't make sense does it?"

Journey didn't know if it did or not, but she was willing to let it sit in her heart. It felt good, and those were things she held onto when she wasn't sure about much. "It's starting to. This is all so different for me, Mama. It feels like I'm breaking out of a chrysalis after a long sleep." Now, Journey laughed. "That probably doesn't make sense either."

Lucille patted her knee. "It makes a lot of sense. You're right in thinking of yourself as something recreated and beautiful beyond description. I think what you're doing is brave and incredible. It's something all of us do at some point if we want to live a life we're proud of." She paused.

"Do your friends know much about your life, Journey. Your life ... before?"

This was another thing bugging her, itching under her skin like a chigger for days now. No matter how honest she had been with Ruby and Cody, keeping her past a secret felt like she was lying to the people who had come to mean the most to her. Before, she'd kept it to herself as a protection, but now, it just felt dishonest.

"I haven't told them yet. Initially, I was scared," Journey hesitated, putting her face in her hands for a long moment, "but now, I'm just not sure how to say it without feeling like a total fake."

Lucille nodded. "I can see where you're coming from. But I hope you give Ruby and Mr. Blake a bit more credit. When God blesses you with these kinds of people in your life, you do what you should to make things right, and you'll be surprised by the help you get."

Journey looked over at her. "Like heavenly intervention. Is an angel going to come down and explain the whole thing for me?" She was just teasing, but Lucille grinned.

"From what I collect, your grandma had quite a love for you. I don't have any doubt she has some pull in heaven to help you in this endeavor."

The goose bumps again. Journey laughed up at the sky. Oh, Grandma. Maybe Lucille was right.

"You're *the* Isabelle Atkins?" Ruby was growing pink in the cheeks, waving the towel she held to cool herself down. Journey took up the same action, letting Ruby ingest the idea and chew on it for a minute. Pink to white and then back to pink. "*Isabelle Atkins* is my best friend," she finally said in a faint whisper.

Journey nodded in agreement. No fainting. No cursing. This was going ... well.

"Isabelle Atkins." This time it was a squeak. "I've fed her, hugged her ..."

Journey put up her hands. "Ruby, focus for just a minute. That girl that you know from the award shows and concerts, I'm her, only... reformed. Think of Isabelle as a costume I wore. The blue hair and eyes, it's not who I am. It's not the real me. This is."

Ruby leaned forward, a lock of her pink hair falling onto her forehead. "Did you lip-sync?"

Journey laughed. "No. I can sing. For real. But I'm more of a country girl at heart. You'll see tonight."

Ruby clapped her little hands in front of her in delight. "Are you saying I'm getting a personal concert from Isabelle Atkins?"

Journey put both her hands on her friend's shoulders. She was perched on the edge of the counter like a five-year-old. "It's just going to be one song from me, but yeah, it's just for you."

Ruby gave her a bashful look and then hugged her. "I can't believe I'm best friends with a superstar!"

When she could breathe again, Journey pushed her friend back. "A superstar who is in hiding, right? You can't tell *anyone* about this."

"No one." Ruby was shaking her head obediently, and then she winced. "Not even my mom? She's not even on social media."

Journey shook her head. "Not even your mom."

Ruby made the motion of locking her lips. "Okay, no one. So ... why are you in hiding, anyway? I mean, I've read all the latest gossip columns, so I could tell you all about it. The top three theories at least. And where you've been spotted and with whom. I don't want to name drop but the hottie you've been hiding with starts with an E and ends with an "Lvis," but *I* didn't say it." She giggled. "Now that I think of it, the alien story might be a little off."

Journey barked a laugh. "Yeah, I think you're right. Really, it's about being the real me. Isabelle Atkins turned into Helen's creation."

Ruby's brows drew together in a scowl. "Helen's a piece of work, let me tell you."

Journey nodded with a broad smile. "Don't I know it."

Ruby's face brightened when she remembered. "Yes you do!" She squealed.

"I just felt like I wasn't being true to who I wanted to be. My grandma taught me better. So, I cut ties and jumped ship. I've been here ever since, getting ready to come out as a country singer with all new representation and totally different life goals."

"Oh my goodness, this is way better than the magazines. I wish I could read this book, I really do." She paused and looked up with a blush. "Especially the kissy parts."

Journey blushed too. "Ruby Whitaker!" After smacking her on the shoulder, Journey grinned again. "I could not have found a more amazing friend. I feel so fortunate that on my first day of scrubbing toilets I'd never peed in, I got to meet you and your wonderful cinnamon rolls. I feel really blessed to know you."

"Me too," Ruby agreed. "And it's not even because you turned out to be a superstar. I liked you before that." Now there were tears sparkling in her eyes. They hugged fiercely, and then, sniffling a little, Ruby asked, "Not even my grandma?" Journey shot her a look, and she locked her lips again.

"Okay, let's celebrate."

"It's breakfast time, Rubes."

"I know," she said with a knowing smile, "and yes, it's not even September yet, but I couldn't resist. I had to try this new recipe, and you're the perfect guinea pig."

Journey looked uncertain until Ruby went on. "Pumpkin Waffles. With syrup and hand-whipped cream with just a *dash* of nutmeg." She rubbed her pointer and thumb together to demonstrate the nutmeg application.

"I'm in," Journey said instantly. Oh, if this could only go as well with Cody. She had a sinking suspicion she might actually need that angelic intervention.

The gathering room had been transformed with a simple stage near the fireplace and a disco ball hovering from the ceiling, casting glittering lights and reflections all around the room. Two microphones and a karaoke machine sat nearby, filling the room with familiar melodies that flooded through strategically placed speakers.

"This is a pretty legit setup," Cody said, rubbing his hands together.

"You've missed this." Journey walked up to him, sliding her arms around his waist and into his back pockets.

He grinned down at her, taking a kiss before agreeing. "I didn't know how much until the music went on. It's been a while since I've felt that beat. I do miss it."

Journey hid a worried look. She wondered how he would feel when he realized she was the girl who'd dumped an ice cold drink into his face last year. But that wasn't her only worry. She worried about the real world with Cody Blake, cowboy superstar and playboy. What would he be like when he was back in the wild instead of the protective environs of Snowflake Falls?

"What?" He had noticed. Light blue eyes looked down on her, taking in her face with a warmth that made her want to forget her worries and draw him in closer. Instead, she wrestled with the right words.

"Just ... wondering what it will be like when you go back."

"Me too," he answered quickly. "To be honest, I'm nervous about how it will all go down. I've been in touch with my attorney and my agent. Ian is my friend so he's totally on board. My agent ... let's just say when I told him about the changes I wanted to make with my music and image, there may have been a bunch of expletives in that conversation." He let out a sigh.

She brushed a curl off his forehead and stood on her tiptoes so she could cup his chin between her hands and press a kiss to his lips. When she sank down again, she tugged his shirt front. "You are amazing. Any label would be lucky to have you singing songs from your heart. Don't let anyone tell you any different."

"You're very convincing," he said, his voice a rough whisper.

"Mmm ... let me convince you some more," she answered, leaning into the next kiss, her arms going around his neck as he pulled her closer. She was in pure bliss until Big Ben cleared his throat behind them.

"Sorry to interrupt," he grumbled, a hearty smile on his face.

Journey's cheeks went from flushed to beet red in lightning speed. "Sorry. We were just—"

"I know just what you were doin'." Ben chuckled. "Just passin' through."

He went through the room and out the back door. Journey and Cody parted, grinning at one another. Journey turned back to him, gripping a flash of insane courage in her hands before speaking. "Cody, wait. I need to tell you something."

"Yeah?"

Her words froze in her throat at the sound that cut through the air next. Like a lightning bolt striking out of clear blue sky, three words flashed brilliant white on the scene.

"Isabelle Jane Atkins!"

Chapter Eleven

Her old name ripped through the air, shrill, harsh, and completely unexpected. Without thinking, Journey's head whipped around. But even then, her eyes couldn't seem to comprehend what stood in front of her.

A woman, with the same build as Journey herself, stood with the air of an offended queen at the edge of the gathering room. Her outfit was runway ready, and there in the rustic beauty of the inn, it looked ridiculous. Her tan was flawless, her dark hair was cut at an edgy line that fell around her jawline, and her dark brown eyes were disguised with green contacts one shade too bright to be real. In the crook of her arm, a purse hung, and from the opening, a little dog face poked through, the color of Ruby's fresh whipped cream.

Beside her stood a tall, angular gentleman in a pinstripe suit. On the other side of her, the one Journey knew she determined was her best side, was a guy with a camera and one more person wielding a reflective shield tilted at the right angle for ideal lighting on the woman's face.

Helen Atkins was standing in the gathering room at Snowflake Falls Inn, poisoning the air with her overwhelming perfume. She'd found her.

Journey's mouth was open. This *was* unexpected. Almost five months, and she hadn't heard a single word from Helen. Living her life without one text, demand, or guilt trip had been unexpectedly freeing. Journey hadn't realized how much she'd relished her freedom from that connection. She felt herself freezing up, her shoulders crunching up toward her ears, her stress level spiking like Mt. Everest. It was only Cody's deep voice in her ear that snapped her out of it and made her remember who and where she was now.

"Who. Is. That?"

Journey stepped in front of him, her protective instinct kicking in, her determination shoving its way to the surface. She was ready to go head-on with this little parody of a domestic terrorist, fluffy white dog and all. Why couldn't this exact moment have happened only a half hour from now? Her stomach flipped when she realized what Cody would think when this showdown was over.

"Go into the kitchen quick. Stay there until the cameras leave."

She said it over her shoulder, while planting her feet and narrowing her eyes at her mother. She didn't get to see the mix of confusion on his face. She felt him hesitate and then, noticing the camera, hurry out of the room.

"What the hell do you think you're doing? And before you answer that, don't think that the amazing publicity you've stirred up for our family business with this charade is going to save you."

Helen Atkins' voice had never been called melodious, and now, with her in full warrior mode, she was beyond shrill. Journey saw her cameraman cringe. It must be worse at ground zero.

All Journey felt was a growing embarrassment, for her mother and for the life she had lived before leaving the city. How could she have stayed for so long and let this woman control her?

"Helen."

"Don't *Helen* me. I want to know what you think you're doing. I am *not* someone you walk away from, Isabelle. It's taken me over five months to track you down, and don't think I didn't feel like giving up would be far more beneficial to our family than this."

She looked down her nose with a sneer. "What have you done to yourself? Sunken to the level of every average girl? I wouldn't even recognize you on the street."

"Exactly. That's exactly who I am. An average girl who is going to do amazing things on my own. My exit from your life is perfectly legal. All my commitments have been fulfilled. I'm out of the family business. Period."

Helen snorted. It was terribly unladylike, but she was losing her polish, her eyes bulging more with every moment Journey didn't come cowering back to her.

"You'll be out when I *say* you're out."

"No," Journey raised her voice to say the word, then lowered it carefully, "I'm out when *I* say I'm out. I'm not coming back. Take what you have and go with it. I won't vilify you in the press if you leave me alone."

"Who do you think you are?" The sneer marred her carefully applied lipstick. Journey was surprised she could even make that expression on her face.

"I'm my grandma's girl," Journey said it firmly, "and I'm going to be true to me."

"Your grandma? That woman you think is such a saint? Ha ha! Well you didn't know the woman who raised me. In fact, it's because of her that I'm here."

Journey felt her hands start to shake. "What are you talking about?"

"In her will, Isabelle. She knew she'd denied you the benefits of life with your sisters. When her will was settled, she'd granted you an inheritance dependent on five years of working with the family business. You are two years shy."

Journey's eyes darted to the man standing next to Helen. He nodded solemnly as if to confirm this statement. But it didn't make sense. Grandma never had anything nice to say about the Atkins Dynasty. Why would she want Journey to be a part of it? Did she realize what she was asking?

"Whatever conniving success you're trying to do with our fame won't work without me. I demand a cut, 50% of all proceeds and 30% legal control, and I'll sign on the dotted line in two years, granting you whatever freedoms you demand."

"My life has nothing to do with you anymore," Journey said, her voice faltering as she struggled to process this new information.

"Ha, as if that would change anything. The Atkins renown will always follow you, and I should be compensated."

Journey shook her head. "No." Helen was right. No matter what she did, her life would always be connected to her mother and sisters, but she was not going to let Helen have even a toehold of control, much less that outrageous sum in profits.

"Think about it, Isabelle. You need a backer and money to get this so-called new life going. There was no love lost between my mother and me, yes, but she always wanted you to know your sisters better. She often mourned the fact that you had grown so far apart. She left you everything you could possibly need if you only fulfill the terms." Here, she paused, snapping her fingers at the gentleman in the suit. He quickly produced a document and held it out for Journey to see. "Sign the document or lose your inheritance and disappoint your beloved grandmother. Success always grows out of money, Isabelle."

Journey stared at the paper, her head swimming. Something didn't feel right. Her mind was racing through all their past conversations. Her grandmother had mentioned her sorrow at seeing her granddaughters grow apart. But Helen had said there was nothing left to her when Grandma died. The land, the house, everything in it ... all sold within weeks of her burial.

"How can that be right?" she wondered out loud.

"Just sign it, Isabelle!" Her mother's voice could have shattered crystal. Journey looked up, her dark eyes centered on this woman who had been her mother. The thought of two more years under her thumb was inconceivable. She couldn't do it, not even for Grandma.

That's when her angel appeared. Jenni walked in with Constellation on her hip. If her mother looked ridiculous, Jenni was the smokin' hot girl next door. Long blond curls tumbled over her shoulders, glowing skin, minimal makeup, and full red lips. Stella was all darling blond curls and a thumb in her mouth. Large blue eyes followed the happenings in the room with careful consideration. When Jenni spoke, her words were thunder.

"Helen, stop!"

Helen turned, as did everyone with her, the guy with the reflector scrambling to keep her perfectly lit, the camera still recording.

"What are *you* doing here?" Helen's hard edged glare began to crack.

"What do you think? Izzy, don't believe a word of this. The truth is, Helen has been hiding the real inheritance Grandma left you. Remember that beautiful old house and all the land you cried over when she told you she'd sold it? Well, guess what? She can't. That land, the house, and every last thing in it is yours by law. And I have the proof."

She held up the legal documents for everyone to see.

"What?" Journey felt her eyes filling with tears. Could it be true?

"How dare you!" It was like an episode of any daytime drama with Helen as the victim.

"I'm going to make you this offer one time, Helen. Believe me when I tell you it won't come your way again." Jenni lowered her burning gaze on her mother. "You leave Izzy alone, or I'm right behind her, with Stella and all my designs and my makeup line."

Helen gasped dramatically, but this time, her face had faded of color. "You wouldn't dare! I made you!"

"No," Jenni straightened and her regal beauty glowed through in that moment, "I made me. You helped me, you made some connections, but I have always done the dirty work and suffered the results of your carelessness. How could I have ever agreed with you about Colin? Those were the most miserable days of my life, Mom. You can't just make contracts for vital relationships and order people around. This isn't the Mafia; it's our family!"

Helen's face was becoming an unnatural color with a flushing in her cheeks and a pale sweat on her brow. "Turn it off!" She screamed at the cameraman. He fumbled the camera, almost dropping it in his haste to cut the video.

"I can't believe you would talk to me like that."

"I should have said it years ago. I've suffered through hell because I wouldn't stand up to you, but those days are long gone." Jenni's voice was a growl. "I don't care what you do on your own, but from now on, my business is mine."

"I get a cut." Helen snapped.

"Fine. But it'll be according to *my* terms. And as long as you leave Isabelle alone."

"Alone. Like she will do anything *alone*." That sneer appeared again, but it looked weak and sickly now.

"She can do anything she puts her heart to," Jenni shot back, squeezing her daughter to her, "and she'll be amazing at it." She put out her arms and Journey hurried into them, her hands shaking. There was something so comforting about holding onto her sister and feeling Stella reach for her, tiny arms closing around her neck and fussing with the edges of her dark hair.

"Izzy." Stella patted her cheek.

"Hi, baby girl." Journey grinned into her sweet baby face.

"I won't stand for this. My own daughters treating me like a cast-off."

"No, Helen," Journey looked up from her niece, "you've used us as your meal ticket for long enough. This is business. You don't get a piece of me, and you don't get to have a say in my life. You stay out, or you'll end up losing everything."

"Liz would never desert me," Helen growled.

"Yes," Jenni examined her nails carefully, "Liz has always been your little minion, but think of how horrible it will look when two of your daughters bail on you and start shining some light on your less than ethical choices. Who do you think will come out on top then, Helen?"

Helen blanched, her composure slipping entirely. "You ungrateful witch!"

"Eighteen months of hell on earth, mother. You made me do it and I will never forgive you. Push me on this, and I'll make you pay."

Journey squeezed Stella, wishing she didn't have to see this. She caught sight, just then, of her best friend in the kitchen. Ruby looked beside herself. She was almost grateful she didn't see Cody's face. A streak of shame ran through her. This was a daytime talk show nightmare, live and in color. She couldn't imagine his reaction to this hot mess.

Helen's shoulders caved in, and for a moment, it looked like she might reconsider her outrageous demands. But that moment was fleeting, and the next one replaced any look of remorse with a towering, superior sneer. Journey saw her then for what she truly was. A person who was lonely and hurt, who had no way of dealing with real emotions because they hurt too much. Her mask of perfection was so firmly affixed, she didn't even know how to shift it.

A swell of compassion found her heart even as she watched her mother order her legal counsel and film crew out the door. It was there that Helen paused to cast one dark look behind her. There was no love in it. No sense of loss or longing for family. It was merely the look of someone who'd lost big and regretted it. Without a word, she was gone in the slowly setting sun of a country evening.

ఇ☙✾✾✾ɞɑ

He watched her from the kitchen, staying out of sight of that damn camera and fighting his own inner battle. He'd twice had to stop Ruby from barging out there with death in her eyes. She was beside herself, pacing and then stopping to hear better. He heard whimpering and a few choice words being muttered under her breath. But her curiosity always won out.

Cody felt outrage that was delicately balancing between covering his identity and protecting the woman he loved. Another part of him was remembering. He recalled a night of personal embarrassment that still made him cringe just thinking about it.

The Country Music Awards Festival in Las Vegas, NV. Isabelle Atkins was a guest musician. She sang pretty fantastic country, in his opinion, though it wasn't her genre by a long shot. When she walked out onto the stage in all her blue-haired, blue-eyed glory, he was stunned by how incredibly hot she was.

Once she had finished her performance, he left his date at the table and headed backstage. He met her in the hallway before she could make it to her dressing room.

"Great work out there," he crooned. He had learned quickly what the ladies liked, and he put it all into play that night. Tight jeans, snug T-shirt, deep voice. Only, her response was nothing like he'd expected.

"*You.*"

That word alone should have set off warning signals in his brain, but three drinks in, he was nowhere near a place of rational thought. He was all bravado and stupidity. He never even saw it coming.

"You're Cody Blake, the new country bad boy, am I right?"

His smile widened. Oh, man, he was reeling her in. Up close, he could tell her bright blue eyes weren't natural. He wondered what color they were when the contacts came out, or did they ever come out? More than that, he wondered how it would feel to kiss those full, beautiful lips.

"That's me, sweetheart. I wanted to congratulate you tonight. Your voice was right on."

"Wow. Thanks. Coming from you, that's something between a slap in the face and a compliment."

He didn't notice the camera sneaking up beside them, but she did. She turned on a quick smile, and he was stunned for a moment. Fake hair or not, she was gorgeous. The glitter on her eyelids seemed to float a little. Maybe he'd had more than three drinks.

"I'm sorry. Didn't mean to come across rudely."

"Well, good thing for you, I *did*. You, Cody Blake, are the reason country music can't have nice things. And as much as every country girl would like to slap you in the face for being such a blatant douche, I'll just have to do *this* in the name of country music lovers everywhere." With one quick move, her drink—ice and all—was in his face. And she was gone. The camera panned quickly from Cody to Isabelle's retreating figure, the feathers on the back of her skirt fluffing with each brisk step.

Cody played off his shocked embarrassment for the camera with a smile and a shrug while he shook out his jacket. A leather jacket, now that he thought of it. It was a mad ten minutes of changing and blotting before he got back out to his table. All night, he had looked for her, her words revolving in his mind, his agent scrambling to maximize the publicity and swing it in their favor. Country bad boy takes one in the face for bad boys everywhere. He could still remember the stupid interviews he'd done, laughing about how bad boys get a bum rap.

Now, he felt like an idiot. He should have remembered her that first day. She had been just as obvious about her dislike of him at the inn, from the very first moment he'd met her.

And then the thought hit him. Yeah, he'd done his research, and Isabelle Atkins loved to pull publicity stunts. In fact, just a few months ago, she'd disappeared without so much as a note. Her social media accounts deleted. *This* was where she went. And if this was all about publicity, maybe ... no way. Was this some kind of deal with her mother? Was this some revenge plot to reel him in and then dump him on live TV? If it wasn't, why had she lied to him the entire time about who she was?

He was an idiot. A complete and total loser, so starved for female affection that he'd fallen for her, just like that. His head sank down into his hands as waves of disbelief fisted in embarrassment hit him.

He hadn't been pretending when he held her in his arms. He hadn't been pretending when he told Ben and Lucille he wanted to do things right. He hadn't been pretending when he hauled her on his back down a fricken mountain, more worried about another human being than about himself for the first time in way too long. He could still feel the warmth of her kiss just before that woman arrived.

Ruby was flapping her hands, looking like she might burst into tears. "That's Jennifer Atkins. She's … ohmygoodness ohmygoodness, I think I might faint!"

"Sit down, Rubes."

She did, putting her head between her knees. "She's only the supermodel of the sisters. Goodness, she's gorgeous, even off the magazine covers. Breathe, Ruby. Breathe!"

She was right. The woman who walked in last was stunning. Gorgeous blond hair, long beautiful legs shown off just right with the cut of a high-end dress. He would have been at her feet only a couple months ago, but now, his vision was different. He ran a hand over his face while patting Ruby's back as her breathing started to steady.

That woman, Helen, he thought, had a voice that could cut through wire. He couldn't figure out how Journey could be the child of someone so obviously cold. He could feel it from here, the chill in her every move that spread across the room like creeping smoke.

Journey was definitely not cold. Or was she? If she was playing him, that was as cold as it got. He shook his head. He couldn't do this. He couldn't do it, because for the first time in weeks, the desire for a drink gripped him hard. Something to take the edge off this feeling in his gut like he was getting kicked and doing nothing to stop the blows.

"Ruby, you gonna be okay?"

He crouched down, trying to focus on something else but knowing he had to bail, and soon.

"I think I'll be okay," she said from somewhere between her knees. "I don't feel like fainting anymore. Are they all still there? I can't believe I'm missing this."

"Don't worry, I have a feeling the whole world will know about it in a couple hours."

Cody cleared his throat, grabbed some sodas out of the fridge, and left. He wouldn't get drunk, but he did think having something to swig would help, even if it only gave him a sugar high.

The back door slammed, and he didn't try to muffle it. He was ticked, confused, and on the verge of heartbroken. The only thing keeping him from driving down the mountain and never looking back was the 64 hours he still owed Ben and Lucille.

Chapter Twelve

Journey ran her fingers through the silky baby hair on Stella's head, entranced by the motion and her niece's steady breathing. Settled there on her chest in luxurious sleep, Journey felt sure she would never move again. They were ensconced on the couch in Journey's cabin, the sounds of friendship weaving their way around the room. Ruby and Jenni were an instant connection, Ruby leaning in for all the details, and Jenni giggling softly at her rambunctious, hilarious ways. Journey was more convinced than ever that there wasn't a person on the planet who couldn't love Ruby.

"Cody held me back when Helen brought Grandma into it. Oh! I wanted to …" She made claw hands, and Jenni chuckled again.

"The way you wrestled that camera guy to the ground was pretty impressive." Jenni giggled.

"I couldn't let him post that video with Journey's personal information all over it." Ruby shrugged.

"Deleting that video was your most heroic feat to date. I totally owe you one." Journey agreed.

"I can't believe how she twisted the inheritance around to suit her," Jenni said, her voice hushed when she looked over at her sister. "What did she think would happen in two years?"

"This." Journey motioned to the baby in her arms. "Maybe she thought having kids would make me settle for her version of reality."

"Then she knows nothing about motherhood." Jenni tossed her head. "It has been the single motivating factor in my life. The reason I get up in the morning is snuggling in your arms right now."

Journey smiled, her heart swelling with gratitude for Jenni's timely arrival. "Thank goodness for my guardian angel."

"Yeah, your timing was incredible. I almost hyperventilated, but I was still lucid enough to see you walk in and totally put the hammer down." Ruby made a karate chop movement that had them all giggling.

Jenni just shrugged. "She had it coming. The question is ... now what? This place will be crawling with reporters by morning. We may have destroyed the video, but let's be honest. She's not going to let you stay here in peace. She'll make as much of this as she can."

"I have to go," Journey said quietly. She'd seen Cody's back when he walked out. His shoulders were stiff, and she could only guess what the look on his face would have told her. And she knew why. All this talk of authenticity, and she'd blown it when it mattered most. Such crummy timing!

"I hate that," Ruby murmured, her face falling into a sad pout. "How am I going to go back to life without this girl? Without the drama and fun and … you?"

Journey's face sank into a frown of its own. The idea of leaving Ruby felt terrible. But it wasn't just her anonymity that was being blown. Cody had little chance of finishing out his time here without the world knowing it. "Maybe if I go, we can redirect most of the blow," Journey said. "Cody is so close to finishing his time here. I wish I wasn't the one messing it all up."

"I know." Ruby look uncomfortable and then blurted out, "He was really upset. It was hard to tell at first if it was because of Helen or me almost fainting, but even with my head between my knees, I could tell he was really bothered by something else. I think it's bad, Journey. He should have been here by now. I mean, you guys were like making out every second this morning."

"Not every second." Journey's cheeks burned red, and her sister grinned. But then, Journey slowly rose from her comfortable position on the couch, cradling Stella in her arms. "You two want to pack for me? I'll see if I can fix this thing with Cody."

Jenni came over, scooping Stella into her own arms and then laying her on the bed, snug as could be with a flannel blanket resting over her. She turned back to Journey, setting a slender hand on her shoulder. "Isab—I mean, Journey. If this guy is half of what you say, he's going to figure it out. But hey, don't be too discouraged if it takes time." Jenni rubbed her shoulder and then squeezed her close, whispering in her ear. "It might help if you weren't wearing a shirt with baby drool on it."

Journey stepped back, examining the trail left on her blouse. True, but if she was going to be real, that authenticity started here. If a bit of drool was too much for him, he wasn't her guy. The thought struck her hard in the gut, catching her reply before she could make it and hurrying her out the door. She didn't have much courage left after that face-off with Helen. She mustered the frayed shreds of what remained and stepped out onto the porch.

Crunching steps in the gravel, hurrying along a path that had known their paces so often in the last couple months, she slowed, taking a deep breath of mountain air. It felt like standing on the bridge in the city all over again, but this time, she wasn't running away from her old life. She was making a choice about where she wanted to be.

The sunshine had fled, it's warmth sucked away to leave an edge of cold to the air that touched her nose and made her shove her hands into her pockets. Tipping her head back, she looked up into the sky, pine trees and quaking aspens rimming her vision. The deep indigo blue was spotted by stars glimmering down at her. Her lungs were soon full of pine-laced mountain air, and deep inside, she knew she would miss this place like crazy. Not just the fun she'd had here, but the mountain itself and the transformation that came in the sheltering care of a little cabin.

She would come back. Maybe this would be where she would write her new albums, or celebrate Christmas with her family one day. Ruby said Lucille went all out for the holidays, and she could imagine these mountains dressed in snow. It would be breathtaking. Whatever happened, Snowflake Falls Inn would be a second home, as would the people. She had to find a way to keep in touch with Ruby, Lucille, and Ben. Her tummy ached a little thinking of being apart from all the people in her life who had made it so rich.

And then she was there. She slipped around to the back side of the cabin to avoid the glow of the cheery twinkle lights beaming into the darkness and the possible camera lens of intrepid photographers out for the money shot. With one last breath, and a prayer for courage, she stopped at the window.

Three small taps.

Would he answer?

Nighttime leaked into her insides, first filling her lungs with cold and then seeping through her veins. She had a feeling that, despite their bright beginning, this was one star that would fall, leaving a crater behind that she would struggle to fill for years to come.

Three more taps. A disturbance of blinds, one blue eyeball, and then footsteps. She reached the back door just as he pulled it in, quietly, and only an inch.

"I can explain."

"You don't need to."

Ugh. Her courage faltered.

"Cody, I was going to tell you."

"When, Journey? Or is it Isabelle? Hell, I don't even know who you are."

"Yes ... you do."

"Really? Because the last time we met, your plan was to make a scene. To humiliate me. And it worked. Everyone thought it was a hoot. What was it this time? Hunt me down in disguise, make me fall for you, then dump me on live TV? When was the big reveal, huh?"

His words were coming out bitter, cynical, angry. They bit and slapped against her skin, weapons designed to hurt her back.

"You know it's not like that. I've been upfront about everything—"

"Everything? I didn't even know your real name until today. We've been working together for almost two months."

"Cody, slow down. I'm not here to hurt you."

His face flayed her open, the burn of hurt in his eyes already lighting up to a bonfire. "Look, *Isabelle*. I don't have time for this. Because right now, what I want more than anything is to find a bar and forget I ever knew you."

Journey felt the blow for what it was. It almost made her turn away. This was what she had feared from the beginning. This wasn't her fight, and she couldn't make him want to change. She stepped back, shaking her head. Maybe this ending now was for the best. She was turning when a thought pushed itself to the top of her mind. "Say it!" It was Grandma's voice, bold and insistent.

Digging deep for the right words, Journey turned back, willing her Grandma's brave heart to carry them.

"Great. Go for it, Blake. You've spent the last five months picking yourself up, dusting yourself off, and becoming a person you could be proud of, but don't let *that* stand in your way. You know where to find what you want. Go get it.

"Just remember. If it didn't happen today, there would be a day—whether you date the perfect person or someone who happens to have a bit of a dark history like me— where they'll disappoint you or do something that will rip you apart whether they mean to or not. And you'll have the same damn reaction. Your old demons will come roaring back, and you'll think you deserve that drink.

"So, if you're going to do it, do it! No one can make you stay sober but you. Whether you believe it or not, I care about you. But I can't make you stay clean either. If we're done, fine. I'm not going to beg you to let me explain. But for the love of all that is holy, wake up and be a man about it. Life sucks. We don't get to run away from it in a bottle. If you're hurting, hurt. If you're angry, feel it!"

There were tears on her cheeks now, but she dashed them away, turning for one minute, and then, without thinking, only knowing that she wanted one more time, she rushed toward him. A flick of her boot shoved the door open wide. His dark hair was a mess, blue eyes bright with his own tears. She stepped toward him, pushing herself up on her tiptoes, fingertips gripping the front of his flannel shirt just like that night under the stars. She would remember how soft the fabric was for days to come. But his lips were softer, and that would capture her memories for so much longer.

Her mouth was on his, fervent and caring, wishing he would understand and put aside his anger to let her explain. In that kiss were all the words she couldn't say and that wouldn't make a bit of difference until he wanted them to. When she pulled away and left, there was a cry in her throat. She didn't see the stunned look on his face or the way he reached after her but then stopped himself, fists clenching to his sides.

೫⃟✻✻✻ೕ

"You sure you're ready?" Lucille's hand in hers brought tears to her eyes.

"No. This place has been so special to me." Journey clasped Lucille to her, grateful for the warmth and comfort that came with a person who had helped her make hard decisions and given her a safe-haven.

"Well, don't go talkin' like you won't be back. Don't be a stranger. You've always got a place here. And not as the help. As family."

Ben leaned down to accept her hug and chuckled as he lifted her easily off her feet. "We're gonna miss you, Little Bit." He pressed a kiss on the top of her head, and Journey felt her heart squeezing. Part of her resented her mother for butting in and forcing her hand. The other knew that the right timing usually felt wrong and uncomfortable when it was driving you out of your comfort zone. That was Grandma's take anyway.

"The right timing always feels awkward. Oh, it's grand to think about, to plot and plan. But when it shows up on your front steps without warning, you start to think maybe it wasn't such a splendid idea after all. That's when it counts. When you dig into the part of you that remembers what it felt like to know it was right. Hold onto that and you'll get through."

Now, she felt like she'd munched up a goblet for dinner instead of Ruby's delicious masterpiece. Now, she needed Grandma's wisdom and a little of the Atkins fortitude too.

Ruby's hug was fierce. "Promise me you're coming back and talking lots in between. I can't even handle the thought of not seeing your face."

"Me either," Journey confessed. "You've got my number now, and don't worry, I'll keep you up to date until you're sick of it."

"Fat chance," Ruby laughed. "Don't you know anything about me?"

They both laughed then. Jenni's goodbyes were far more reserved, but that was just Jenni. While getting into the car together, with Stella in the backseat looking extremely alert for a baby at midnight, Journey let her eyes stray to the dark outline of her home for the last five months. She loved that shadow, especially the peak in the center where she could see the outline of the lights and the dear little porch where she had set her foot with intention every morning.

But she loved the one beside it more, or perhaps more honestly, the man within it. How she wished he were here, taking her hand, holding her tight, and saying he would be with her through the challenges ahead. But he wasn't. And she needed to be okay with that if she was going to move forward. So, she closed her eyes, mentally filling the air around them with a thousand kisses that would never happen, and turned away.

In the last five months, she'd left her family twice, but this time, she felt the tender unseen cords of connection that made her watch the inn until it was swallowed into the darkness of the mountain.

ഇ✵✵✵ര

A broken slant of light fell over Cody's face, shining bright, angry moonlight into his eyes in an act of rebellion. Even the moon was ticked. He had tried a thousand times to turn over and go to sleep. His goal at the start of the night was to forget everything he knew about Journey Miller/Isabelle Atkins. She'd shattered that idea to pieces by showing up, getting in his face when he tried to be an idiot, and then leaving him with a kiss that knocked his socks off. He wasn't going to be forgetting that anytime soon. Not in this lifetime. Nor would he forget the look in her eyes (dark pools of intensity), the way her hand went to her hip when he'd talked about drinking, and the tears that slipped like crystal drops to her cheeks and made him ashamed to be the man making her cry. Again.

Here he was, again.

Back to this point.

Ashamed of who he was.

Journey had been talking about life purpose and doing something bigger all week, her eyes full of something he couldn't ignore. There was a passion there that scared the crap out of him and made him feel like maybe he just wasn't good enough for this girl.

Life purpose?

He had never considered more than his own fame as a goal for his life. Self-promotion had become second nature to him with all the pleasures that it brought. But she was right. The emptiness of looking out for oneself caught up quick.

While Journey had been brainstorming with Bel about sustainable clothing, wells in underprivileged communities, food banks, and other reputable ventures, he'd been hanging back. He had to admit it to himself now. He had already been looking for a reason to pull away.

Because he didn't know if he could be the kind of person she wanted him to be.

He didn't know if he could give that much of himself.

Now, he could see that it wasn't her that he was angry with. It was him. What the hell was wrong with him?

He got into a kickboxing death match with the sheets on his bed and landed on the floor, puffing hard. What *was* wrong with him? His mother had taught him to be a giver. They had done community service whenever they'd had the chance. She was always telling him that when the good Lord blesses your harvest, you find a way to help the less fortunate.

They'd spent many a late summer night helping a neighbor in need. It was the bread and butter he was raised on. Why was he so afraid of saying yes to this idea when everything that came with it was so appealing and made him feel amazing? He loved everything about that girl. Her passion when she knew she was right made him push himself.

He stood up too quickly and had to steady himself on the bed. What had he been thinking? Suddenly, with his anger melted away, there was a sticky residue of guilt in its wake. He had been a complete idiot at the inn.

When Journey was being confronted by the Wicked Witch of the West, he'd gone all flying monkey and joined the throng of persecutors. He'd walked out when he should have been backing her up, taking the hits for her, telling her mother where to take her threats. He sank down again with his head in his hands.

Oh, man, he had blown it. Big time. Big Ben said to show up when it mattered and he'd tucked tail and ran.

The minute he'd started thinking of the past, he'd let it cloud his vision of who Journey was now. He'd only seen the girl she was pretending to be back then. He was an idiot to have thought she could be anything different than what she'd shown him in vivid color. In the last two months, he'd seen her fierce loyalty, her snarky sense of humor, her unwillingness to back down when things got tough, and her passionate, intense emotions when she was all in.

He wiped a hand over his face with that last thought. He was a fool. He had accepted his last girlfriend, warts and all, and was grateful, even, for her flaws. Completely willing to live and let live. Mostly because it let him relax his own ideals. And now, when he'd stumbled onto one of the best things he could ever imagine, he was rooting around for faults.

He was on his feet the next moment, hurrying out the door without thinking to grab a sweater. The summer nights were quickly giving way to fall, and there was a bite of chill that goosebumped his arms. Maybe it was the feeling in the pit of his stomach that he'd just made one of the biggest mistakes of his life.

Her light was out. But no, it wasn't just that. There was a vacant feeling to the very air around cabin 4. He walked closer and realized it was empty.

His heart started racing, keeping pace with his legs as he sprinted to the inn. Dark.

To his surprise, Lucille was still up, sitting behind the front desk looking a little forlorn. Her clear blue eyes didn't hold a note of surprise when he busted through the front door with the grace of a moose on a rampage.

"Where is she?"

A lifted brow. "Are you looking for someone, Mr. Blake?"

Gasping. "Journey. Where is she? The cabin … is empty."

Lucille took a deep breath and tried a smile. He didn't like the looks of it. "Left a few hours ago, Cody. I'm sorry."

"What?" He threw up his hands, pacing to the door two steps and then back, his hands on his hips. "Where? I need to talk to her. I didn't even …" He grabbed his cell phone, screen still shattered. He hadn't even thought to get her number. There was so much time for everything this morning.

"Cody, we don't know. She's got some things to finalize before she can come out in the open again. You must know how difficult her mother is after this afternoon."

Cody shook his head, that sinking feeling he'd had in his stomach congealing into a solid rock. "You have to know where she went, Mama. Come on. Give me *something*."

A look of compassion and a fleeting sadness tugged at his heart. "I wish I did. Journey thought it would be best if we didn't have to keep secrets anymore."

He let out a bitter laugh. Secrets. Boy, they'd had their share, hadn't they? He settled onto a chair in the entryway across from the desk and hung his head.

"Then what do I do?"

There was silence. He appreciated how Mama Lucille didn't rush to answer the tough questions. She leaned back, her eyes taking on a far-off look. "My daughter got herself into some trouble with her husband a couple of years ago. A mama knows when things aren't quite right. I had that feeling under my skin for months, but there's a fine line you walk as the parent of a grownup, ya know?" He nodded, wondering for a moment how this had anything to do with his question.

"When Ben and I heard the depth of it, we were fierce. If he was the bear, I was the lion. We both wanted to attack, swoop in, and tear that guy to pieces." A wry smile. "I guess that's where we learned something about maturity. And letting God do the fighting. We had to wait until she was ready to walk away and find her way back to us. Sometimes, you feel like running after someone; sometimes, you need to wait for them to come to you. Now, I don't know which one you should be doing, but I think the Man upstairs has a bit of an inkling. Maybe you need to rush out and find that girl. Maybe you need to wait a bit. I guess I'm saying, you'll know in your gut what to do, but first, you gotta be willing to trust it."

"My gut has not been the most trustworthy advisor lately," Cody admitted, "but I hear what you're saying. I just messed it up, and you're right. I want to rush in and make it better."

"You know, Journey used to go to the bridge when she needed some counsel," Lucille said with a warm smile. "She talked to her grandma there. I think she'll always find a way to be close to Grandma June."

Cody nodded. The bridge. Past the mud puddle where she creamed him the first day. Past the lake where he felt just how cold mountain water could be. Past a dozen trails he walked with her, wondering how he could get lucky enough to win her smile that day.

"Thanks, Mama."

"Mmm hmm," she hummed, fingering a paper in her hands. On it was a date in September when her girl would finally be coming home.

Chapter Thirteen

Sunlight kissed the mountaintops and washed Journey in its rays, coloring her in the end of day.

"I am *so* glad you said you would come." Journey's cheeks hurt from smiling so much. She relished the company after a month on her own, writing, recording, working with her new band and agent non-stop, and making Grandma's house her own.

Ruby leaned forward, the end of her short curls tinted a mermaid blue. "Are you kidding? You called, and I was out the door before I packed." She paused then, out of the side of her mouth, said, "Speaking of that, I may need to borrow some underwear." She made a face and then went on. "I was so excited. Of course, Dante is over-the-moon at the idea of running the show on his own for a week. Good grief, that kid is gunning for my job. But ya know, it feels good to know the inn is in good hands when I have to be away, luxuriating in the country with my superstar friends, especially now that I can know your address. You're pretty good at keeping secrets, ya know?"

Ruby's dimple was infectious. Journey tipped her head back and laughed, her dark hair falling in waves over her shoulders. Being alone had been therapeutic in many ways, but it had been awfully lonesome too. Grandma's house, now her own, was different without the shining personality and companionship of Grandma June.

"Can you believe this all happened in a month? The house, my agent, the band, the music? My first show is in six weeks, and I still can't believe it's really coming together."

Ruby watched her for a moment while selecting a slice of fresh apple from the tray between them. "Are you sad, ya know, to leave *Isabelle* behind for good? I mean, you were that girl for 23 years."

Journey thought about it. "You know, I wondered if I would be. Changing my name officially was sobering. But the real me has always been a country girl living in my grandma's house. Taking the name Journey Miller kind of felt symbolic. Part of making a clean break. There's just no way I'd ever be free of the Atkins drama if I didn't." Journey shrugged, taking a slice of her own. "In reality, I'll never be free from that connection, even with a new name. But I did want a chance to start fresh."

"I'm proud of you. I think I'd be too afraid of failing to unhitch from the Atkins star." Ruby said. Her honesty made Journey nod.

She knew just what Ruby meant. Dropping her fame wasn't as easy as picking it up again. She was risking a lot by cutting ties with her famous family. Her dark eyes searched the scene around the old house, the peeling white picket fence that needed a fresh coat of paint, towering old trees dressed in the colors of fall, and piles of autumn on her lawn.

"Oh, believe me, I've been worried. Working with Home 4 Dinner helped me shift my perspective. Making sure these kids have dinner every night after going home from low-income schools, well, it's bigger than me. There's something about it that makes me feel like I'm a success already."

Ruby grinned. "That nonprofit is incredible. I had no idea kids went home to nothing."

"It's terrible to consider, isn't it? While the lunch ladies cry over the leftovers they're mandated to throw in the dumpsters? Yeah. Such a crime. Until the government gets that figured out, we're going to fill the gap." Journey looked at Ruby with determination. Ruby beamed back. They both chewed for a minute, letting the silence stretch itself between them while looking through the large plate glass windows into the house.

"This place is really coming along."

"Can you tell? I'm going for a balance between the old stuff Grandma collected and my own personal touch. I was stunned to come home and find all of Grandma's possessions still here. I thought they were long gone." She pointed through the glass at a piece in the kitchen. "That hutch has been in her family for a hundred years. The victorolla is an old-fashioned music player her mother passed down."

"Good thing you like antiques." Ruby pumped her brows. She fiddled with an apple slice for several seconds before peeking over at Journey. "But we both know what I'm really dying to ask you about …"

"Cody Blake?"

"Yes! Any news?" Her face was split between expressions of hope and fear.

Journey looked down, studying the old Converse sneakers she scuffed against the floor. If she were being honest, all this busyness was a direct effort to keep her mind off Cody and how much she missed him. The excitement of her new life was enough to distract her, even just a little.

"Nothing, really. Honestly, I haven't made it easy. I've been in hiding from the public until the notices of concerts went out last week. I changed all my personal info and kept it out of my feeds. All my social media platforms are managed by my assistant for now. Cody never even had my number."

These were the hopeful excuses she told herself. She hadn't reached out to him either, though she was no longer using an old flip phone, and she would admit she'd searched up his agent's number and almost dialed it a thousand times. What made her punch the call cancel button again and again was not knowing if he would want to see her.

When she left the inn … well, he'd been pretty clear about how mad he was. At this point, she didn't know if he'd relapsed or worse. In some ways, she didn't want to know. She wanted to cherish that memory of their time on the mountain, that kiss on his back porch.

Ruby's hand on hers brought her back. "You need chocolate; I can see it in your face."

"Ruby, I had to start running because of all the goodness I ate on the mountain."

"I'm only here a week," Ruby countered. "And if I'm not mistaken, that's a new range in there?"

Journey grinned. "I thought you might notice. I just had it delivered last week. Grandma's was this old '70s harvest gold number. Those are double ovens on the wall, too."

"You're going to love me in about two hours." Ruby's hands emphasized her plan. "Until then, I need some time with your pantry."

"Go for it. If I don't have it, Marva next door will. She and Grandma swapped all the time."

"Got it." Ruby was already tuning her out, her ever-present humming kicking in as she made her way to the kitchen. Journey heard the drawers being opened and closed as Ruby acclimated to the new cooking space, then, "Apron?"

"On the hook inside the pantry door," she called back.

"Genius! Okay, you going to watch or what?"

Journey laughed, bringing the empty plate inside and rinsing it in the porcelain farm sink.

"You know what? I'm going to take a walk. I've got an hour, right?"

"At least. Maybe two, depending on how crazy things get in here."

Journey paused on her way to the front door. "Ruby, don't burn my house down, m'kay?"

Ruby looked up from tying on the ruffled apron. "What do you mean?"

Journey sighed. "Fire extinguisher is under the sink."

"I can be careful."

"I know." Journey grinned. "See you in a few."

Humming met her in response with the clink of dishes being pulled out and the clatter of a set of measuring spoons hitting the counter. Already, the house seemed more full and alive than it had only the day before.

Journey pulled open the front door, grateful for the way it still stuck, just like before. She could almost feel her grandma nearby, walking with her on her way to the cemetery.

Her town was big enough to boast a scrap of a main street, but Journey's house was out far enough into the country that she didn't encounter much more than a tractor on her way down the lane. Her glance stretched over the hill, and out toward the edge of town where the headstones caught the evening light in a way that made her catch her breath.

It really was a beautiful place to rest.

It didn't take long to descend the rise and find her way to the gate. Rustic lawn stretched over the cemetery, carpeting everything in its path. A groundskeeper did his best to keep things neat and tidy. She found Grandma's stone, still as fresh as the day it was laid there almost four years before now. She looked out over the markers, thinking.

"She loves it, just like I knew she would," Journey told her grandma. "I think you'd love it too. It's so nice to make those improvements you always thought about but never did. Thank you for the house. I know I said it before, but ... I can't thank you enough. I finally feel like I'm home. Home for good."

She scuffed her sneaker in the grass, wishing for a moment that she'd thought to toss on a sweater instead of leaving the house in her baseball tee that read: "FARM GIRL." She traced a finger along the rough edge at the top of the stone. "Sometimes, I think I see him from the corner of my eye. This one guy—who works at the car shop in town—has the same beard thing Cody wore." Journey bit her lip. "I miss him so much, Grandma June. And I thought by now ... I would know what to do about it. But I don't. I just feel this emptiness, and nothing, not the music, not the concert dates, not even helping these kids has filled it."

She felt the sadness of that first night and driving away from Snowflake Falls settling around her shoulders all over again. Wrapping her arms around herself, she fought the urge to let the tears flow. Thank goodness for the distraction of a pickup driving up to the gate. It was one she didn't recognize—a navy blue truck with a dented side fender and dark tinted windows. Puzzling over who the driver could be was just the mystery she needed to help reign in her emotions. She had learned the art of watching for the tale-tell glimmer of a camera lens. A hand on her brow to block the sun's last rays, she observed the truck from afar.

A guy got out on the driver's side. Baseball cap, jeans, and a flannel shirt. Nice build. She looked down. "Nice, Grandma. I don't need any eye candy right now, seriously." She rubbed her arms, wishing for her sweater again. It wouldn't be long before the trees would finish shedding their leaves and leave her with nothing but bare branches until spring.

"This the Gunlock cemetery?" The guy was calling from the gate. The sun was at his back, casting him in an unhelpful silhouette.

Journey put a hand on her hip. There was an arch in metal—hand welded by Mr. Klacker's son—that said "GUNLOCK CEMETERY" in large block letters stretching over the man's head. She pointed at the sign and the guy looked up. Did he look familiar? The angle of the light made it impossible to tell. Her heart sped up, nevertheless. Traitor.

Considering the number of times she'd mistaken dark-haired, bearded men in her small town for Cody, she was pretty sure she shouldn't get her hopes up.

The gate opened, and the guy walked in, a bouquet of flowers clutched in one hand. Hat, sunglasses, beard, really great build. Hmm ...

Journey stopped herself from admiring him. Looking familiar didn't mean he was who she hoped. She wondered, instead, whom he might be visiting.

Her eyes wandered the graveyard. "Any new friends of late, Grandma?" But there were no new mounds of freshly dug earth. It often took old Mr. Duncan about three weeks before he got the new plots sodded.

She watched him follow the path through the headstones. Maybe she shouldn't be so nosy, but the truth was, she was curious.

His pace had slowed, his face taking on an expression that made her stop pretending not to look and stare right back.

"I wonder if you could help me find someone?"

"Depends on who's lookin'," Journey found it hard to be casual. That voice was definitely familiar. The closely trimmed beard. Those lips she would recognize anywhere.

He took off his hat and there were the lush dark curls. The sunglasses weren't far behind, revealing light blue eyes and a smile that would have stopped her heart anywhere.

"Cody Blake."

"Journey." He stopped a few feet from her. The look on his face said he was taking in the moment, drinking up the vision of her, and puzzling out what to do next. She had a hunch he wasn't confident he would find her here.

Finally, she blurted out, "What are you doing here?"

He shook his head with a wry twist of his lips. "It took me a month to get it. Mama Lucille said something about you always wanting to be close to your grandma. I could remember Gunlock from our conversations and started searching for any Junes in the town graveyard from there. The whole time, I was afraid to find you and terrified I wouldn't."

His blue eyes found hers, wary, gauging her response.

Night had taken hold of the sky, shushing the sun in a blush that flushed to the mountains and stirred up the fireflies. They started to wink in the backdrop of the fields around them. Journey shook herself, wondering if she was dreaming or if Cody was really standing in front of her. How many times had she hoped for this moment? Now, she didn't know if he was here for closure or something more.

When she didn't say anything, he held out the flowers, a bundle of daisies, chrysanthemums, and carnations in bright colors that she accepted, touching them to her nose and breathing in the pleasant aroma.

"I brought these. For your grandma. Just in case she was the only one I got to talk to."

"Thanks …" Journey gently placed them on the base of the stone, touching the letters that spelled her grandma's name before she stood again.

"If you ask me to go, I will." His face was stoic, and she knew he was hovering somewhere between hope and resignation.

She tried to smile. "I don't want you to go, Cody."

He let out a pent-up breath. "Journey, you're all I've been thinking about. Since the minute I let you walk away. What a terrible idea."

"Wait. Cody, I need to tell you something. I wish I could have done it at the inn, but everything happened so fast."

Cody nodded, waiting, his eyes fastened on hers. His stance reflected a willingness to hear the bad news and anxious desire to stay.

"I should have told you everything: about being Isabelle, about hiding, and about my family. I'm sorry you had to find out in such an awful way."

"Wasn't your fault," he said.

"Yes, it was. I needed you, but I didn't trust you enough to tell you. I wanted to, but I hesitated until I ran out of time." Journey felt the frustration again at her mother's horrible timing before dismissing it.

"I wish I'd been a better friend, Journey. I shouldn't have left you standing there."

"What happened after I left?" Journey knew most of the story from Ruby, but she was still curious about his side.

"You can imagine. A whole contingent of lifestyle reporters. More than a few fans. I left for the city again by the end of the week, and the judge commuted the rest of my sentence for good behavior."

She nodded. "I'm glad it worked out and sorry that everything had to change."

"Not your fault," he repeated. Then he took a step toward her before retreating. "I was a mess." He shook his head. "I had a big fight ahead of me. Turns out, you were right about rough times happening when you least expect them. Coming home wasn't easy. Old friends, old habits ... they were waiting there for me."

She nodded, her heart sinking. His eyes looked clear, but maybe she was missing something.

"It took me a few weeks to really clean house. The old crew ... they thought maybe it was just a phase. Heck, I even wondered if it was." He chuckled darkly. "But one thing kept coming to my mind."

Journey looked up again, meeting his eyes. "What's that?"

"When I'm with you I want to be a better man."

She searched his face. "Is it enough?"

"You're enough. You're ... everything."

He took that step again, this time with intention.

"One month without you was enough to solidify a couple things for me, Journey." He took another step, and she held her breath, desperate to know what his next words would be. "My sobriety is not a phase. Every good thing in my life has happened since I let go of that crutch. And my life is seriously jacked up without you."

She started to cry then, the silent kind of weeping that fills your eyes with tears and shakes your shoulders. He saw it and his composure slipped.

"I don't want to do this alone, Journey. I could spend a thousand years apologizing, but I'd rather hold you in my arms and tell you the words I kept inside on that mountain."

His look, now, was for permission. She could only nod and open her arms as tears streaked her cheeks. He closed the distance in one step, scooping her up against him, her cheek brushing his. His grip was so fierce it stole her breath and lifted her from the ground before easing. She sunk back to the earth as they both sniffled.

Pulling back, his eyes were the most beautiful sky blue. "Please forgive me for being an idiot."

She nodded again. "I already have."

"Journey, I don't just need you, I want you. I've never wanted anyone like I want you. To be my friend. To hold me to my purpose. To hit me upside the head when I'm in the wrong. To cheer me on. I want your spunk and your sass. I want every curve of your beautiful body. Please tell me we can try again."

He untangled enough to use the pad of his thumb to wipe the tears from her cheeks. It was a futile effort, though. She was far from done with them. Not after holding them in for so long. She let her hands travel up to his face, softly caressing his jawline, soaking up the vision of his smile.

"I keep having this dream that when the fireflies are out, you come back to me," she said, her voice catching. "Every night, I've watched. A whole month. 30 days that felt like they would never end. I've liked boys before, Cody Blake, but I have never wanted to slug someone the same day I've wanted to kiss them until my lips went numb." She ran a finger over his lips and felt him shudder against her. "I've missed you. The way you hold me, the sound of your voice, the way we fight and laugh and love. Yes, to trying again. Yes, please!"

He closed his eyes then, relishing the sound of her acceptance. She took that as an invitation to tug him down and reacquaint their lips. It had been a long absence and they both needed a refresher course on why they loved the whole idea of making out.

Cody's hand moved to cradle her neck and turn her head to just the right angle. The steadiness of his arms around her, the feel of his heart racing against hers, and the warmth of his kiss all told her he had no intention of letting her go any time soon.

There might have been a few blushes from the angels watching from the other side, but Journey did her best to kiss him for every day they'd been apart ... and then a few extra.

They spent longer than planned at the cemetery, and when the dark blue truck pulled up in front of Journey's house, Ruby was watching on the front porch as the tall cowboy came around and opened the door, letting Journey slide off the seat and into his waiting arms. There was a whoop that could be heard to Martin's general store, and Ruby was probably already planning their reception dinner in the back of her mind.

སྐ་❀❀❀ལྕ

Journey's first concert had been a success. She thought back on it in moments like this, when she was nervous to her toes.

She could still visualize the front rows of fans, their cowgirl hats bobbing and boots stomping to the rhythm the whole night through. Her favorite part had been the acoustic set when she sang her new single with just her guitar and the voice God had given her. Perched on a barstool in a gown that flowed with ruffles down the skirt, she'd told the audience her story.

"My grandma taught me that life is about living out loud. For a while, I tried being what everyone else wanted me to be. But today, this is the real me, the real color of my hair, the real color of my eyes, the real sound of my soul. I wrote this song a few months after walking away from everything that broke me down. I want you to know that being authentic is probably the biggest leap of faith you'll ever take. If you do nothing else, be brave."

The words flowed then, with her guitar as backup.

"Hands on the wheel
Not lookin' back,
I'm leaving everything behind.

Broken apart
Cutting all ties
Not tellin' anyone goodbye.

I'm leaving you
And all the past behind
What's old is new
I'm takin' time to fly …"

Looking in the mirror now, she saw that her dark hair had grown in the few months since she'd given that speech. It flowed over her shoulders in gorgeous waves done with skill by her sister's hairstylist. Her gown fell around her bare feet while she let her sister put the finishing touches around her eyes.

"You look stunning," Jenni said, her finger lifting Journey's chin so that she looked up into her sister's eyes. "I mean it. I'm jealous. Of this," she motioned to Journey's gown, cinched in bustiere style on top and flowing with layers of tulle skirt below, "and everything else. Cody is really amazing. I'm so happy for you, kid."

Journey grabbed her sister in a fierce hug. "Jenni, I know there is someone out there for you who will love you like Cody does me. Only better. Because you deserve the best."

Jenni laughed through the tears gathering in her eyes. "I believe you. Thank you. For letting me be a part of this. I understand the secrecy, and I support it. But I don't think I could handle missing one more important part of your life. I feel like it grounds me whenever we're together. The fact that Stella adores you helps a lot too."

"You're a part of my life, Jenni. For good. I would never get married without you."

A knock at the door found the sisters squeezing each other tight, tears threatening to destroy a good half-hour of makeup artistry.

"Thought I'd find you two like this." Mama Lucille entered, followed by Mrs. Blake, her dark hair curling nicely around her jawline.

"I brought reinforcements!" Mrs. Blake announced.

If Cody had worried for even a second about his family accepting Journey, his fears were completely misguided. His brothers loved her. His sisters-in-law immediately bonded with her over shared stories of loving the Blake brothers. And his nieces and nephews fought over the tiny space on her lap at every occasion.

But perhaps the greatest connection was between his mother and Journey. They took to one another like old friends. Mrs. Blake, or Laura, as she insisted Journey call her, held nothing back from the new love in her son's life, especially when she could see the profound change in him. He'd come home a different man, a heartfelt apology the first thing from his lips. As the weeks wore on, Laura learned about his time on the mountain and the affect Journey had in Cody's life. She knew Journey was instrumental in his transformation, and her mother-heart was forever grateful.

Laura entered the room now with a tray of delicacies, including a protein bar chopped up into slices for easy ingestion.

"Let me guess: haven't eaten all day, feeling weepy, and on the verge of happiness overload?" Laura slipped a hand around Journey's waist for a quick hug. "You look far too fabulous to give in to tears. What you need is food and quick. What looks good?"

Journey's tummy answered with a growl almost in unison with Jenni's. "Okay, maybe you're right." She started with a deviled egg and almost cried anyway. "Mama, how does she make them so good?"

Lucille, who'd been watching with a misty look of pride in her eyes, shook herself out of her emotions and gave a grateful shrug. "You know Ruby. She's always sprinkling things with her magic."

"Try this." Journey turned to her sister and didn't wait for her to refuse.

"Wow." Jenni's eyes went wide.

"You're never going to fit into your zeros when you get home," Journey grinned, "and believe me, you'll like it. Boys like it too."

Jenni grimaced at her. She still wasn't used to eating too much, but Journey was working on her.

"Now, I've got a very nervous groom downstairs, a pathway through four inches of fresh snow, and about thirty really great looking guests hoping that Ruby's food is as good as they've heard. Are you ready, little Journey girl?" Lucille's gorgeous red hair was arranged in beautiful curls around her head, her clear blue eyes matching the dress she wore, and her smile brilliant in the light of the room.

Journey took a deep breath. "I'm ready." And she was.

They'd been dating for only a few months, far too short an engagement by modern standards, but they both felt the truth of their love deep inside. What Journey wanted more than anything was to spend the rest of her days with this man. She couldn't see any reason to spend another night apart.

They made the plans and kept them simple. A Christmas wedding at the place where it all began. Not

Vegas, but Snowflake Falls Inn, with the people who mattered most braving the snow to gather in an intimate ceremony where Big Ben would officiate, Cody Blake would sing a song he'd written just for her, especially now that he was writing from the heart, and Grandma would look down and smile.

It was far too cold for fireflies, so Jenni made sure there were antique Edison bulbs of all shapes draped around the yard and throughout the trees that rimmed it.

Walking down the stairs in a pair of honey leather cowgirl boots, she met Ruby who was dressed in robin's egg blue to match Jenni's gown. Their wedding party was small, their guest list short. Ruby joined Mama Lucille, and Cody's family on the front row. The five B sisters were also among the guests. Though the media caught wind of Cody and Journey's relationship, there were no official announcements. Not even their agents knew they would exchange vows this weekend. In fact, they were completely off the grid for the whole event.

Journey took a deep breath. Amongst her grandma's old things, she'd found a gold ring with four small diamonds. It fit on her right ring finger and made her feel like Grandma was walking her down the aisle, just like she'd hoped. With the memory of Grandma close to her heart, she took Ian's offered arm on one side and Jen's on the other to escort her through a walkway garnished with crimson petals.

Journey relished the moment. The brisk bite of winter air. The festive pine garlands on the aisles. Pine and holly berry wreaths. The glow of twinkle lights warmed the air, but it was nothing compared with the zing of attraction that swirled around her between Ian and Jen. When she saw Cody at the end of the pathway, it was all she could do to keep her pace and not rush into his arms.

Later, she would remember the color of his eyes when he looked down into hers. She would recall the feel of his hands clasping hers while they said the words that meant forever. In the years to come, she would think fondly on the kiss that made Ruby squeal, and on the way Cody pulled her against him and kissed her again. And her mind would always linger on the way he looked when he took his guitar and began to strum the strings. The song he wrote for her brought tears that would not be stayed. That was a moment she would treasure forever.

When the cake had been cut, the bouquet thrown (and caught by none other than Ruby Whitaker), the dancing until the wee hours done with relish, Journey would remember the rush of goosebumps that spread up her arms when Cody lead her away from the lights. He gathered her into his arms, her dress making the endeavor infinitely more difficult than it needed to be. But he was built for the task. When he carried her over the threshold of Cabin 5, she knew she was right where she needed to be.

The End.

Journey's Hit Single - Drive

Drive
Hands on the wheel
Not lookin' back
I'm leaving everything behind

Broken apart
Cutting all ties
Not tellin' anyone goodbye

I'm leaving you
And all that's past behind
What's old is new
And I'm takin' time to fly

Hands on the wheel
Looking ahead
I'm reinventing my old life

Breakin' away, finding my truth
I'm growin' wings
and now I'll try

I'm not afraid
Of the girl that's in the mirror
Her open heart
Is the way to find my truth

The day has come to run after my dreams,
It's time to fly!

Taking the wheel
Not gonna cry
This is the way to live my life

Embracing the truth
Setting me free
Lovin' the freedom and the strife

I've come to know
That it's not where you have been
It's all about
The woman that's within

And so I'll drive.

Cody's Wedding Song - There's Somethin' Beautiful

There's something beautiful
About the way your heart meets mine
There's nothing typical
I'm always so surprised.
You never say just what I think you will
Or let me get away with, the crazy things I do.
There's somethin' beautiful, it's true.

There's somethin' amazing
When you touch my hand.
It's drivin' me crazy.
I'm needin' you so bad.
Your perfect sense when it all goes wrong.
The way you calm my mind, and help me to be strong.
There's something amazing, this time.

You caught me burning bridges in my past.
Playing games and music that would never last.
You rescued me with nothing left to find.
And helped me see the future, one day at a time.

There somethin' that stuns me,
and takes my breath away;
It's the way that you love me
And make my heart feel safe.

This day will be remembered all my life,
The day you said u loved me and became my wife.

There's somethin' beautiful….it's you.

Cheesecake Brownies
Recipe adapted from Allrecipes.com

Ingredients
Brownies:
1 (18.3 ounce) package brownie mix – your favorite box mix with the eggs, oil, water for mixing it up.

Cheesecake Topping:
2 (8 ounce) packages cream cheese – softened
2 eggs
2/3 c. white sugar

Directions

1. Prepare the brownie mixes together and as directed on package instructions. Preheat oven to temperature indicated on box. Grease a 9x13-inch pan or line with parchment paper.

2. Spread brownie batter evenly in the prepared pan. Using an electric or stand mixer, beat together the cream cheese, egg and sugar until smooth and creamy. Drop the cream cheese mixture by spoonsful on top of the brownie batter. Swirl together using a knife or skewer.

3. Bake according to manufacturer's instructions for a 9x9 pan (as your brownie mix will be thicker and re-

quire more baking time). Brownies will be done when a toothpick inserted 2 inches from the edge comes out clean. Cool in the pan. Cut into bars and serve.

4. Refrigerate leftovers.

*Ruby would want you to know that these bars are very tasty after being refrigerated.
*Ruby cut these bars into small bites for her guests, but you might need to eat them in the larger bars.

Creamy Chicken and Wild Rice Soup

Ingredients

¾ c. uncooked wild rice blend
1 c. chopped onion
1 c. diced carrots (2 medium or 6-8 baby)
1 c. diced celery (2-3 stalks)
7 T butter, diced and divided
1 clove minced garlic
4 ½ c. chicken broth
¼ t. each dried thyme, marjoram, sage, and rosemary
Salt and ground black pepper, to taste
1 lb boneless skinless chicken breasts, cooked and shredded
½ c. flour
1 ½ c. milk

Directions

1. Prepare rice according to package directions. Set aside.
2. When rice is almost done, in a separate large pot, melt 1 T. butter over medium heat. Add onion, carrots and celery and sauté until slightly tender, about 4 minutes, adding in garlic during last 30 seconds of sautéing. Add chicken broth and spices. Bring to a boil and then reduce to medium-low heat. Add cooked rice and shredded chicken to soup.

3. In a separate medium saucepan, melt remaining 6 T of butter over medium heat. Add flour and cook 1½ minutes, whisking constantly. Continue to whisk vigorously while slowly pouring milk into butter/flour mixture. Cook mixture, stirring constantly until it thickens. This is your roux. Add the roux (milk mixture) into the soup in pot and cook about 5 minutes longer or until soup is thickened. If the soup becomes too thick, add a splash or two of milk, water or chicken broth to desired creaminess. Season with salt and pepper to taste.

*You can also use white rice or any other rice for this soup. Just precook and stir in whatever you have on hand.
*Ruby would feel free to mix up the veggies in this soup. Good swaps are finely diced broccoli or zucchini.
*This makes about 5 servings. Double if you're expecting a hungry group.

Panzanella
Adapted from Pioneer Woman

Ingredients
1 loaf crusty baguette
1 whole cucumber, peeled, halved, seeded and diced
1 ½ dry pints of cherry tomatoes (Ruby likes red and yellow mixed)
½ red onion very thinly sliced
¼ c. olive oil plus more for drizzling on bread
1 T red wine vinegar
25 whole basil leaves washed, stacked, rolled and thinly sliced
Parmesan shavings
Salt and pepper

Directions

Preheat oven to 275 degrees F. Cut the bread into 1-inch cubes, arrange on a baking sheet, and drizzle lightly with olive oil. Place the pan in the oven for 20-25 min. to slightly crisp the bread without toasting it. Remove it from the oven and allow to cool.

In a large bowl, combine bread, cucumber, tomatoes and onion. In a small jar, shake together the olive oil, vinegar, salt and pepper. Pour over the salad ingredients, tossing gently. Add basil and Parmesan shavings and toss again. Cover and allow to sit at room temp for an hour or two before serving.

Sprinkle with salt and pepper. Serve.

*This is one of those recipes you can't make at the last minute. You need prep time to toast the baguette and allow the dressing and tomatoes to mingle once tossed together. So don't wait! Make it after lunch and it'll be ready for dinner.

Acknowledgements

The more I create the more gratitude I feel for a Creator who is the Father of all things. I am so very grateful for the access I have to a portion of His creative genius and for the blessing of this outlet in my life. I hope that God will always be the one I thank the first and the most. Without Him, I would have nothing. With Him, I am everything He needs me to be.

I want to express a big thanks to my husband and kids who brainstorm, listen to me babble about fictional characters and their problems, and who put up with mediocre dinner menus and subpar housekeeping while I am in the creative zone. They're seriously the best.

My editor, Emily Carter, is so talented in this and many other ways. Her genius put to work in my favor helps me to relax and do what I do best. Thank you friend!

If you could gather a bunch of authors together, make them friendly, genuine, spiritually grounded, hilarious, goofy and really great to hang out with, you'd have my beta readers. These people have made my world more colorful, fun and blessed. In their presence I feel so loved. Being with them is one of my favorite places to be. Thank you dear ladies! Kimberly Krey, Ruth Josse, Katie Dodge, Chantele Sedgwick, Jeigh Meredith, Peggy Eddleman, Shelly Brown and Donna Nolan, you really are some of my favorite people!

Special thanks to my formatter, Bob Houston. The name says it all. If he's a Houston, he must be fabulous. He does a superb job on my books and he's great to work with. I recommend his services to all my writer friends.

If I didn't make it obvious, I love music. Country music is a genre close to my heart. Music is powerful. It has the ability to lift a broken heart, mend a hurting mind, and heal the pains that we're afraid to share. I believe in the power of good music. There's even greater power in worshipful music that honors God and praises a Savior that gave His all for us. Searching out and supporting musicians who make the world a better place with their talents will open the door for even more great music. Let's flood the earth with lyrics that inspire peace, love, acceptance and forgiveness. It makes a difference.

To learn more about Christene Houston and her other works, follow her on Facebook: Award Winning Author Christene Houston || Twitter: @writerChristene || Instagram: @Christenehouston || Pinterest: Christenehouston || Christene's blog: Christenehouston.com

Read on for a sneak peak at the first book in the Snowflake Falls Romance series: Cookie Girl Christmas!

Book Club Questions

1. Both Journey and Cody struggle to meet demands and expectations in their lives that leave them feeling fake. Have you ever been in a relationship (family, friendship, work or partnership) where you can't be your real self?

2. Journey rejects Helen's demands to marry for money and prestige. What era does this kind of arrangement remind you of? Can you think of any current celebrity pairings that seem to fit this mold?

3. Journey leaves the city and hides away at Snowflake Falls Inn to get back to her roots. We all need a timeout to get back to basics and align our priorities. Do you ever feel like you're on auto-pilot in your life? In what ways do you nurture your authenticity?

4. Lucille describes an experience where being around a woman living her passion gave her permission to reevaluate her life. Have you ever found yourself initially judging or disliking someone like Lucille did? Once you got to know them, what passion did they give you permission to pursue?

5. Cody uses alcohol to numb the pain of losing his voice and detouring his dreams. How does addiction play a role in creativity? Do you ever stifle your dreams

with a substance or excuse? What simple ways can you give yourself permission to unleash your unique voice?

6. Journey is a huge fan of 90s clean country music. She felt that music should inspire and change you. What are some classic or contemporary songs that motivate you?

7. Grandma June has a lot to say in When Fireflies Sing. What's your favorite Grandma June quote and why?

8. Ruby is the absent-minded culinary genius at Snowflake Falls Inn. What are some of your favorite scenes with Ruby? How did Ruby's friendship help Journey progress?

9. In the ever-growing push for Diverse Books, there is a call for more books depicting characters with religious beliefs that aren't solely for the Christian market. There are numerous mentions of God in this book. Did you feel the author was able to weave in this diverse cultural quality in a balanced way?

10. Bel talks about a life's purpose and Lucille gives counsel on how to find it. What did you think of Journey's effort to pursue her life's purpose?

11. Journey and Cody have a heated conversation before she leaves the mountain where Cody seems to teeter on the edge of sobriety. What did you think of Journey's reaction? How did she put the responsibility of staying

sober back in his hands? Do you think she should have done more to convince Cody to resist temptation?

12. Both Journey and Cody have "sell-out" moments in their lives. How were they similar and how were they different?

13. How was the slip down the mountain a premonition of the challenges to come in Journey and Cody's relationship?

14. We get just a few glimpses of Ian and Jenni. Do you think they would make a good pair?

Now an excerpt from
Cookie Girl Christmas

Chapter One

"Call out the Coast Guard, I think we're out of buttercream." I smoothed a strand of golden hair behind one ear, straightening my apron and searching the room in a careful review. Everything was in order despite the strain of panic running through my nerves that made each twinkle light shine more brightly.

Carefully, I listed things I was grateful for in my mind.

I'm grateful to work with my best friend, even if she's easily distracted.

I'm grateful for the magic of Christmas.

I'm grateful this job gets me one step closer to a shop of my own.

The tightness in my chest eased, and my shoulders sank an inch with each thought.

"You forget who you're working with. We not only have plenty of buttercream, but we also have extras of almost everything on the dessert table." Vee Devereaux, my lovely assistant, rolled her eyes at the typical case of nerves that often set in on demanding jobs. "I can drool over hot boys *and* get the job done all at once. It's why you hired me." Her smile was smug, the one she used when trying to diffuse the anxiety from the air.

When that didn't work, she sighed. "Molls, ya gotta relax. You're tensing up over nothing. These people already think you're amazing. I mean, they've hired you for the entire flippin' season. You're going to pay off the minivan in one fell swoop!"

I ducked behind her, scanning the room for Vanessa Davenport, the wealthy young mother who'd hired me. I shushed Vee with a whispered, "Genevieve, don't talk money at the party!"

"Really? I'm Genevieve now? In case you hadn't noticed, the party hasn't started yet. See, that guy is still slurping cocoa at the counter. Note to self, dark washed jeans look oh so good on a man."

I sighed, "Oh, Vee. I thought you and Jon were still an 'item'."

"Please, you know he's my one and only. I'm just picturing *his* bum in *those* jeans … it's a lovely thought."

I did my best to keep my imagination in check. The last thing I needed was an image of Vee's boyfriend in anything less than a snowsuit. Besides, I was too focused on making sure that things were perfect to be distracted by good fitting jeans. To be honest, I would never have noticed the jeans to begin with. I would have noticed the strong, broad shoulders and the admittedly sexy biceps straining at the sleeves of his shirt. Not that I was looking.

The Davenports were my best clients. An almost monthly stipend of cookie boxes supplemented their generous holiday extravaganza to friends, neighbors, and teachers—all gifts that originated from The Cookie Jar: my bakery and party planning business that promised to have its own store front by late next year. This holiday season, they brought it all up a notch by hiring me as their dessert caterer for an extended welcome home party. A long lost son was revisiting the family manor and reportedly was the cousin of Buddy the Elf in regard to his love of Christmas. Thus, the Twelve Days of Christmas was decided upon, with a new party every other night to extend the celebration throughout the month of December, beginning on the 3rd. I was in charge of the fancy cookies and beautifully arranged tables spread with holiday confections.

Genevieve Devereaux was my best friend and willing partner in these shenanigans. When there were cookies to be made or elaborate tables to be constructed, she was my go-to girl. Genevieve, or Vee as she preferred to be called, had an eye for style and a knack for seeing what I missed. Besides, she was one person who really got me and my slightly manic drive for perfection. She didn't seem to mind that I spent so much time going over each cookie in precise detail. And she understood the constant whispered gratitudes that came out of my mouth when I was feeling stressed.

Like now, when the bloom of panic in my chest told me I had forgotten something important. I just didn't know what.

I'm grateful for Vee's superpower ability to catch my mistakes, even if she has an attitude about it.

"Handmade Santa face cookies, white and green chocolate dipped berries, white chocolate popcorn in paper cones, red and green jelly beans …" I ticked off the items on my mental checklist as I looked them over. The table was Christmas joy on display, decked in red and green with gold touches woven throughout. On this first night of Christmas, when the snow had not yet begun to fall, it could not have been more beautiful.

"What you're forgetting is how crazy these rich people can be. I mean, I've heard of Twelve Days of Christmas, but in my house they involve canned pears and fake birds with feathers falling out—not an actual party train for the month of December." Vee walked around to the back of the table and slowly rotated one of the cake plates holding the dipped berries. Then, almost as an afterthought, she mounted a small letterpress printed card to the front of the plate. In elegant script it read: "Chocolate Dipped Strawberries" with flecks of gold across the white surface.

I gasped, "The name cards! That's what I was missing!"

"Don't worry, girl. I got it." Vee attached the other cards and then stepped back, her black and pink polka dot apron covered in frosting and sprinkles.

I sighed, scanning the table again with a critical eye. "It's flawless," I breathed. And just in time. The doorbell started ringing and that could only mean one thing: we needed to disappear.

"Quick, grab the containers."

Back in the enormous second kitchen we could truly relax—for a moment anyway. Heaven knew our work had just begun. This party would likely go on for hours, and we needed to keep that gorgeous dessert table stocked the entire time.

"I know what you're thinking, and it's not in our contract to waste our whole night refilling the trays," Vee said with a little more sass than was necessary. "They have staff for that. We're only supposed to set up the table and supply the refills."

"But what if …"

"What if they put the berries where the cookies go?" Vee batted her eyes in a practiced swoon.

"Stop, Vee."

"Oh Molly, you need a life, girl."

"I *have* a life," I told her, wagging a finger. "It just so happens I love making cookies."

"Cookies you never eat," she accused. Where Genevieve Devereaux was tall elegance with generous curves and cleavage, I was slender with long legs and way less of that cleavage. A quick glance at my reflection in the oven door confirmed what I knew. The girl who looked back had bright blue eyes and blonde hair streaked with gold that could most often be found in an up-do. A swoop of bangs fell across her forehead, almost hiding a smudge of melted green chocolate. I noticed she could use a bit of concealer under those eyes—due to the lack of sleep that came with baking at wee hours of the morning—and a little lip gloss. Rubbing the chocolate off my head, I sighed and smoothed my apron. Vee was right. What I lacked in generous sleeping habits I made up for in a figure that could take a lot of cookie tastings and still remain trim.

"You know I love to dance."

"Okay, but tell me dancing works off everything you taste."

"That's the thing, I taste, ... I don't do much more. You know what it's like being around sweets all the time."

"Yeah, it's tempting as hell!" Vee shook her head, patting her hips. "Now don't get me wrong, Jon loves a girl with hips, but I could use a little less jiggle in my wiggle."

"You should come dancing with me sometime. It's lots of fun."

Vee sighed, leaning back against the counter. "I'll think about it. Please just tell me we're blowing this joint. I have Christmas shopping to do."

I studied Vee's smooth brown skin as she spoke. It was a perfect cocoa butter color year round that made me slightly jealous. "You go on ahead. I won't stay much longer."

She met this statement with a frown. "Now if I come in tomorrow and you look like you've been run down by a truck, I intend to press charges."

"On the truck?"

"On my best friend who isn't taking good care of herself," Vee said pointedly. "Remember, this is a marathon, not a sprint. We're going to be doing this all month long. Pace yourself, Perfectionist Fairy."

"I'm trying," I said, going back to arranging the trays of goodies that would go in after the first wave of the night.

I heard the door close and let out a deep breath.

I'm grateful for the chance to be a Perfectionist Fairy, even if I endure ridicule.

That brought a smile to my face.

Vee was right. I needed to just go and let the hired help put out the refills. I bit my lip and looked around the room. It was a gourmet kitchen with a huge gas range, double ovens, a farm sink, and a fridge the size of my minivan. The first time I set foot inside, I had the uncontrollable urge to set up my mixer and lay out my cookie sheets. One good hour of baking in this kitchen, where there was room to stack up cooling racks and drizzle chocolate, would have been pure heaven. It was made with a baker in mind.

"You know she never uses it?"

I whirled at the sound of a male voice coming from the entrance to the hall. There stood a guy with the overly scruffy facial hair of someone who'd forgotten to shave for a week. He wore a casual pair of khakis, a shirt and tie, and a sweater vest that transformed him from the dark washed jeans of an hour earlier. I knew it was him. The biceps tipped me off. I wondered vaguely if I'd gotten all the green chocolate off my forehead and if my hastily wrapped hair was as messy as it looked just a moment ago in the oven reflection. Tucking a swath of hair behind one ear, I looked at him carefully.

"Excuse me?"

"She never uses it." He ran a hand through his dark hair scattering water droplets as he did. "She's the queen of takeout. It's a shame, don't you think, with all these gourmet appliances?"

My eyes narrowed. "I think it's a shame to talk badly about your hostess."

"Hostess," he said the word, tasting it. A smirk on his face lifted one corner of his full mouth higher than the other as he leaned his long body against the counter and surveyed me with bold blue eyes. "You're the cookie girl, right?"

I crossed my arms over the bib of my apron and lifted a brow. "The 'cookie girl'?"

"Yeah, you're the one who made all those leering Santas out there?"

I felt a tightening in my chest at the words, and my mouth dropped open. "Leering?"

"And the strawberries suffocating in their "holiday appropriate" colored chocolate?" He made air quotes.

"Suffocating?" I couldn't keep myself from repeating the offending words. He sauntered back toward the hallway with a careless air that had me ready to blow steam out of my ears. "I'll have you know …"

"What, that you hand dipped every strawberry in your pathetic determination to please a bunch of people who are basically unpleasable? Well, don't worry. I'll digest a few handfuls of stale popcorn in your honor. 'Night, Cookie Girl."

He walked out into the hall toward the rising din of clinking glasses and clattering plates above the hum of conversation and Christmas music. His hands were in his pockets, his shoulders relaxed, as though we'd had the most pleasant conversation. I stood there gaping, offended on every imaginable level.

Stale popcorn? Leering Santas?

I whirled to examine the extra cookies, studying them from several different angles. There was no way those rosy cheeks and twinkling eyes could be considered 'leering'!

I'm grateful … ugh! Deep breath.

I'm grateful for losers who keep me humble … and furious.

I slowly loosened my fingers that had automatically balled themselves into fists, and again smoothed my hair back behind one ear in an effort to collect my volatile feelings.

Critics. There would always be at least one. I could handle critics.

I'm grateful for critics who show me what I'm made of.

Instead of busting that guy's nose and ruining his stupid preppy clothes, I would go home, change my outfit, and go dancing. The idea put a lift in my step as I went through the motions of organizing my trays one last time, casting a fleeting glance at the party room, and sneaking out the door.

~*~~*~~*~~*~~*~

"Oh no he didn't. What a loser!"

"I know, right? Can you believe he called the popcorn stale? It wasn't stale was it?"

"We popped it just before tossing it in gourmet chocolate, Molly. Why are you letting him get to you?" Vee's voice over my cell phone earpiece was just as sassy as it was in the kitchen.

"I'm not. I just …"

"He dealt a low blow to a perfectionist," Vee muttered. "Criticize a baker's baking and you've got fighting words. I'm just surprised I'm not dragging your butt out of the slammer for breaking his nose."

I grinned, pressing a hand to my forehead. "What are you talking about? I'm way more mature than that."

"Since when?"

"Look, I'm at the club. Have a fun night shopping with Jon."

"No Jon, just me and the credit card taking a few new electronics for a Christmas test drive."

"Be careful, I know how you and electronics can be," I laughed.

"Look, just because I have a designated jar of rice on my kitchen counter does *not* mean I am a liability with every device that comes into my hands. I've had this phone for—"

"Two weeks and five days," I chimed in, shutting the door of the mini and walking across the street to the dance hall.

"You're betting on how long I can keep it alive, aren't you?"

"Jon is a betting man, and I couldn't resist some easy money."

"Now, that's just not right," Vee said.

"You know we adore you and your crazy quirks."

"Hey, let's remember I'm not the only one with crazy quirks, um kay?"

Before she could go into *my* crazy quirks, I let her go and tucked away my phone. I unpinned my hair that had been twisted into a messy knot at the nape of my neck and let it flow down to my shoulders. I tussled the crown and put on lip gloss. This was Latin night at the club, and I intended to spend the next three hours forgetting about the critic at the Davenport's and reminding myself why I loved the fluid, spicy music, and the moves that came with it.

It was midnight when I took to the parking lot, fanning my face despite the chill in the air. Even though my hair was limp around my face from sweat, a smile lifted the corners of my mouth. That smile had nothing to do with the handsome guys who'd spun me around for a few numbers, but rather the way dancing made me feel.

The strength and spirit of moving to the music was something I couldn't explain. I didn't need a round of drinks to lift my mood, what I needed was music and room to move. It was how I kept fit when faced with dozens of treats every day. Dancing kept me sane while dealing with the pressures of running a business and my propensity for perfectionism.

When I reached my minivan, that smile faltered.

My headlights were still on. A miserable, flickering shade of white reflecting off the night around me.

"No! No … no no no no no!"

I hurried to open the door and slide in, hoping I could preserve what little energy was left in the battery. The inside lights came on but began to flicker as I shoved the key into the ignition and chanted a revised prayer. The battery prayer was actually one I repeated quite often. This was kind of a problem I had. Maybe one of the quirks Vee would have named off if I'd let her go on earlier. Dang it! I'd been talking on the phone and had completely forgotten to turn off my lights. One turn of the key, and the indoor lights went out. The starter churned hopefully only to wind down like a neglected music box. The battery prayer continued to go through my head as I lowered my forehead to the steering wheel.

A tap at my window did more for my heart rate than a spin around the dance floor. My head jerked up, my heart pounding, followed quickly by a lowering scowl when I recognized the face through the glass.

"Hey, you're the cookie girl, right?"

I opened the door, noticing a crowd of guys and girls heading toward the club past my car.

"What are *you* doing here?"

About the Author

Christene Houston is a native of Las Vegas, Nevada, binge reader, music obsessed, mother of 5, ninja writer of YA and Women's Fiction. She loves to write in stormy weather, but settles for busting out words in the persistent sunshine of LV. When not writing, you can find her embarrassing her kids by throwing out old school slang (yo!), recipe testing with her latest victim…er…willing husband, throwing parties that include a flurry of Pinterest hunting, and daydreaming of lengthy trips across the pond to admire the haunts of her fave author, Jane Austen. Her books, A Heart So Broken and Cookie Girl Christmas have lots of great kissing and deep issues where people get hurt and have to figure out how to live through it – kind of like real life. But hey, the kissing! Her newest novel is the second in the Snowflake Falls Romance series, When Fireflies Sing and indulges her love of country music and sassy protagonists. Get your copy on Amazon.

45155854R00161

Made in the USA
San Bernardino, CA
01 February 2017